THAT DARN CAT

THAT DARN CAT

a novel

Janos Toldy

ISBN Paperback: 978-1-7330820-2-0
ISBN eBook: 978-1-7330820-3-7

Printed in the United States of America

Book Cover and Interior Design: Creative Publishing Book Design
Cover Art: Bogdan Maksimovic

To my brother

CHAPTER 1

It was 2012 December 23, a quiet Sunday evening, and Andrew Daniel Foster was watching the LA Clippers play the Minnesota Timberwolves. Andy liked basketball and watched Jerry West, Karim Abdul Jabar, Magic Johnson, Bill Walton, Michael Jordan, Shaq and Kobe play the game, but he never was a true fan. Being an Angelino, Andy liked the Lakers because they were a Los Angeles team, but he also liked football, skied in the winter and loved to watch tennis.

Andy's interest with the Clippers organization started with reading the headlines about Donald Sterling, his mistress and his wife. Andy felt sorry for Doc Rivers coming from the Boston Celtics, to work for a guy whose organization was called The Plantation by the insiders around the League.

The Donald was so out of touch with reality, every time he opened his mouth he made things worse. There was a rumor about the guy being delusional, and everybody worried about the Clippers future. Watching the Clipper games Andy enjoyed the talented bunch, and noticed how the rumors affected the player's performance. As Andy's sympathy grew he learned about Chris Paul, Blake Griffin,

DeAndre Jordan, JJ Reddick and Matt Barnes. On the top of all that they had Jamal Crawford, who was the best sixth man in the League. Winning or losing didn't matter to Andy he believed the Cippers were the most interesting team to watch.

When Donald Sterling was forced to sell the Clippers and Steve Ballmer bought the team for two billion dollars, Andy's interest grew. When he saw the new owner's exuberant sideline behavior it must have rubbed off on him, because Andy was now a Clipper fan.

Holding his chin up with his right knuckles and his right elbow on his right knee, Andy watched Chris Paul bounce the ball to Mat Barns. Mat jumped with the ball arching it over the defender's waving arms, and would have missed the basket. But Blake Griffin flew through the center, snatched the ball from the air and smashed it through the loop.

"Wow!"

Andy reached for his glass of red wine as he watched Blake swing from the basket. He remembered when the Plexiglas shattered under the player's weight, and some of the players got hurt. They must have fixed it Andy thought, knowing the six foot ten inch power forward weighs at least 260 pound.

Mat and Blake waved to each other and when the ball was thrown in the Clippers backed up in defense. A Minnesota player made a mistake by trying to throw a pass over Jordan, and he blocked it with ease. He directed the ball into CP3's hands, and the Clippers switched from defense to offense. Blake blocked for Chris to dribble by, and CP3 sneaked around some of the opponents to pass the ball to JJ Reddick, who was wide open in the right hand corner. JJ jumped with the ball, and at the top he floated, defying gravity, and then flipped the ball into the basket. Andy raised his glass for he believed; the three point jump shot was the most beautiful move in any sport.

Maybe the scissor-kick looks more acrobatic but it's very rare, and only looks good when the ball goes by the goalie, and into the net.

Satisfied with his assessment of the different occurrences, Andy watched Minnesota score twice and that made him edgy. He found the game more interesting when the Clippers were leading by a huge margin. The game was going great when Blake fouled a Timberwolves player and that pissed him off. Andy clearly saw the Timberwolves player push Blake on the floor, but the instant replay show that Blake tripped the guy.

"How did the referee see all that?" Andy mumbled when the doorbell ringed, followed by a knock on the door.

Curiously annoyed Andrew placed his wine glass on the cafe table, and went to see who that would be. Through the peephole he saw the woman from upstairs, who had complained about the volume of his television before. He glanced at the TV and it was not loud, so he waited for her to go away, but she rang the bell and knocked. Hunched over Andy opened the door just enough to look out with one eye, and barked. "What do you want?"

The woman was short and was looking up, and then lowered her view to find him at eye level. "Hi. It's me from upstairs," she whispered. "Sorry to bother you but there's a kitty at your door."

"What kind of kitty are you talking about?" Andy said it with an irate tone, then turned to see what the noise on the TV was about, and watched CP3 steal the ball.

Outside the thunder and lightning made the woman shudder, as she stared at Andy's back. "Can't you hear?" She yelled competing with the elements. "It's been crying at your door for quite sometimes."

Andy turned to her opening the door slowly, and then standing up to fill the doorway with his six feet four inch and a half, lanky frame. "You don't seem to understand," Andy said with an annoyed stare. "The TV's not loud and I really, but really don't want to be bothered." Andy said, slamming the door shut. But she blocked the door with her shoulder, and set her foot into the doorway slot.

Andy stared at her shoulder against the door and her foot in the gap, and with the fury he opened the door wide, and leaned into her face. "What do you want?"

"I've been trying to tell you," she said staring back at Andy." There's a kitty at your door."

"What kind of Kitty are you talking about?" Andy voiced, looking down at a gray little fuzz ball at his feet, staring up at him with a hopeless cry.

"It's a cat," Andy said, backing away. "I hate cats."

"I didn't know that," she shrugged unconcerned.

"I always hated cats, get it away from me."

"I can't do that."

"Well, I'm sorry," Andy said trying to close the door but she won't let him, and then Fuzz Ball joined in with another heart wrenching cry.

Andy gazed into the dark rainy night, with lightning and thunder, and came to realize there's a storm out there. He stared at the defiant woman with her windblown hair, and everything seemed surreal. Andy looked down at the cat with a heart wrenching cry, and wondered if they can train them to do that.

"You're joking, this whole thing is staged," Andy said, watching the tall Italian pines bend in the wind.

The woman shook her head and said. "This is not a joke."

The wind picked up and sprinkled some raindrops on his forehead, and wiping it off with his robe's sleeve it slowly dawned on him; she wants him to take in the damned cat. But Andy didn't want the goddamned thing in the house, but to leave it outside would have been too cruel. Not knowing what to do, Andy took a deep breath and firmly looked into the woman's eyes and shook his head. "Okay, but only for the night."

"Oh well, of course," she said with a relieved sigh, as she timidly removed her foot from the doorway slot. "I'm sure my husband can find a place for the poor thing."

"Are you sure?" Andy asked.

"Of course I'm sure, he knows people," she said indignantly.

"Okay," Andy said bending down to pick up the cat, but his robe almost became undone and he grabbed it to hold it closed. Andy stood up and motioned for her to toss in the cat, and then he slammed the door in her face.

Andy went back to his wine and game and tried to relax but the place felt deflated, like he let the game's atmosphere out the door when he let the damned cat in.

"Where is the cat?" Andy murmured, tracking the odd noise into the kitchen where the kitty was scratching itself in the middle of the floor.

"I should have known you're not alone," Andy said, scratching the back of his neck. "You must be hungry," Andy said looking into the fridge. "Are you thirsty?" Andy said, closing the door. He picked up a stainless steel bowl from the dish rack, washed it then wiped it dry. He filled it with water, and was about to place it on the floor when his right shoulder began to itch. He tried to scratch the spot, and with his awkward moves he scared the cat away. Andy placed the bowl of water on the floor and the kitty slowly approached it. After a short smell the cat begin to gulp like there's no tomorrow, and Andy had no idea how much water the tiny thing should have. When the kitty stopped he grabbed the cat by the back of the neck and pulled it away from the dish.

"I think you had enough," Andy said, lifting it up for a closer examination. The cat was only a few weeks old with soft gray fur, white belly, and white paws. The kitty had a pleasant scent if it would have had a gland to produce it. Andy noticed the cat's left eye was closed, and when he forced the eyelids open with his thumb and forefinger, he saw the gray cataract.

"You poor thing," Andy said, setting the cat on the floor. It was hard for him to believe that someone could discard a small cat, like it was a damaged toy. He tossed the bowl into the sink and the noise startled the kitty. "Sorry, forgot I have a guest," Andy mumbled, patting the cat. It took hem a while to remember the nursery rhyme. "You pat your dog and stroke your cat, and feed green leafs to your turtle pet."

"Tell you what, I go and get something for you to eat," Andy said stroking the kitty. The kitty pushed its head against his hand and Andy couldn't help but smile. He stood up holding his back, all this up and down just didn't agree with him. Andy went back to the living room to check on the Clippers, and felt a lot better when he found out they were leading.

"Holy shit, I'm missing out on a good game," he mumbled, watching the cat fallow him into the living room and then seat on the floor. The small thing looked up at him and squeaked. "Okay One Eye, don't rush me," Andy said, going into the bedroom to change.

He was irritated and slammed the door shut. Andy didn't like unplanned situations, and became worse when he put on his sport shirt turned inside out. He took a deep breath corrected the mistake. Coming from the bedroom the cat was in the way, and with an annoyed stare Andy walked around it. At the door Andy took his raincoat from the wreck and was outside locking the door when he realized, he never liked cats.

Driving to the store the wind rattled the car, and Andy felt the tires rolling over the fallen leaves and tree limbs. It was hard for him to believe that he was out in a blizzard, getting food for a one eyed cat some asshole just thrown out.

On the supermarket parking lot Andy parked near the entrance, and stopped the engine. He pulled up his collar, downed his cap, got out of the car and slammed the door shut. Andy rushed to the entrance, and shaking the water off he looked around and saw only two other cars on the entire parking lot. Andy locked the doors with the remote, got a pushcart and entered the store. It felt weird being in a supermarket in the middle of the night just to buy cat food. Pushing the shopping cart by the aisles he turned into the pet food section, and was staring at the different brands. There was a face of a happy cat on every can, and each one promised a balanced nutrition. They had chicken in gravy, turkey in gravy, beef and gravy and all kinds of fish. Andy learned from the cartoons he watched that cats like fish, so he picked two cans of tuna filets. He heard about cat litter, but didn't know how they look like. Andy decided to learn by reading the labels, and after he gathered all the information, he carefully picked the colorful pebbles cats used in places like the Xanadu and the Taj Mahal. At the checkout stand he asked for a cardboard box and when he was outside he tapped it on the ground to get rid of its tenants.

When Andy got home Fuzz Ball was waiting for him by the door, and followed him into the kitchen. Andy made room for the cardboard box and as soon as the pebbles were in it, the kitty crawled on top poking and sniffing the stuff. Andy washed and wiped the stainless steel bowl and read the cat food label one more time. He tore off the lid and the outpouring scent verified his excellent taste in cat food. Andy found a plastic spoon and was about to scoop the food into the bowl, when he glanced at the small cat. Andy changed his mind and lifted a saucer from the dish rack, and dumped the cat food on the saucer. Filled the stainless steel bowl with water and placed both on the ground.

Andy enjoyed watching the kitty eat, licking its chops then looking up at him with that thankful eye. He noticed the plastic spoon was still on the saucer, so with a shrug and a chuckle Andy stroked the cat with one hand, and removed the spoon with the other.

Back in the living room Andy stopped behind the couch to watch the game but it was over and that pissed him off. He felt being violated, and the whole thing made Andy fill unsafe in his own apartment. Andy got back to his couch and lifted his glass when he heard a weird, scratching sound. Andy placed his glass on the table and went to investigate, and when he reached the kitchen door the awful smell of cat shit hit him in the face. Andy tried to take a deep breath to calm down, but under the circumstances it was impossible. He stared at the kitty in the box, calmly shoving the colorful pebbles with its hind legs. Andy was so furious he didn't know what to think and neither was the kitty, or the miserable thing would have committed suicide.

"How am I going to get rid of the smell?" Andy wondered, watching the small thing climb from the box. The kitty set on the floor moaned, and was glaring at him with that eye.

Andy was fuming and at the same time he tried to be rational. The kitty used the box on its own just the way he intended and the whiff is just part of the process. He was ready to exonerate the kitty but the stench was in the air, and it was getting into his clothes, and when people come to visit will smell the cat. Andy knew the cat was doing what it supposed to do, but one more poop like this and he will never get rid of the stench. Andy unceremoniously picked up the cat by the back of the neck and was ready to throw it out, but when he opened the door the cold, wet wind hit him in the face and he stopped his swinging arm. Andy lifted the kitty and stared into the eye. "We'll smell your shit together."

Andy kicked the door shut, and threw the cat on the couch. He walked around staring at the little stinker, and then he shoved it to the side to take his place in the middle. Sipping his wine and clicking the remote Andy changed to a movie channel where the movie "Topper" just started, with Carry Grant and Constance Bennett. It was past midnight when the movie ended and Andy stood up to yawn and stretch, when he noticed the kitty. The tiny thing was sleeping on its back, with its legs in all directions. Andy chuckled with a smile, then turned off the television and tip-toed away.

CHAPTER 2

Andy shut the bedroom door before he gone to bed, and the next morning the place was cold and damp. He quickly got into his robe and slippers and coming from the bedroom he almost stepped on the damned cat. It was strange for him seeing a kitty in the house, and then remembered letting it in. Andy rushed in the living room to look at the damage, but everything was okay and in its place. Andy felt guilty for being overly suspicious, and picked up the cat.

The small thing was cuddly, and was melting into his arms if the cat had no bones. Andy carried the kitty into the kitchen, and as soon as he got into his chair the tiny thing wiggled onto the table. The cat climbed up on some books to sit on, and looked out the window. The kitty made such a perfect pose, Andy pushed himself away on his rolling chair to take a better look. The noise from the chair's coasters startled the kitty, and it spun around. Andy moved the chair to show the cat where the noise came from. The kitty watched Andy like he was a curiosity, and then turned back to the window. The cat's movements were so feminine Andy thought it was a girl.

"Are you a girl?" Andy asked, but the kitty ignored him.

Andy picked the kitty from the books and placed it on the floor. He checked the saucer and found some dried food in it, so he washed it and opened the other can. This time he poured only half of its contents out and covered the remaining pet food with aluminum foil. When Andy was placing the remaining cat food in the fridge, the kitty was attracted to the shine of the foil, and it gave him an idea. Andy tore off some more aluminum foil from the spool, and squashed it into a small ball. He rolled it on the floor and the kitty chased it down, jumping on the top of it. Andy enjoyed watching the cat play but it was gym day, and he had to get ready.

He went to brush his teeth, washed his face, got into his gym outfit, and Andy on his way out he stopped in the kitchen to see the kitty play. Andy looked around for things that can hurt the cat, and when he saw a knife by the sink he put it away and then he left.

It was a clear and beautiful day, the radio played the overture from the Merry Wives of Windsor and Andy would have enjoyed the three mile ride, but the cat was in his mind. If his neighbor fails to find a home for the damned thing, he will be stuck with a one eyed cat.

Andy was thinking about ditching the kitty at one of the animal shelters, but he didn't like to see caged animals so he rejected the idea. Sam Dart his old neighbor loved animals but he had glaucoma, and Andy didn't think it would be appropriate to dump a one eyed cat on him. Not knowing what to do Andy tried to think of times he spent with cats, and could only remember seeing his grandmother chasing the cat out of the house with a broomstick. Andy's father was allergic to cats, his mother was afraid of dogs, and Andy grown up without any animals around, and he never even had a pet rock.

Andy recalled seeing people walking their dogs, and remembered their faces and the color of their dogs, but as he got older they slowly disappeared and he never knew if they had cats.

"And with time they all vanished," Andy mumbled, and a cold chill ran through him. He shuddered and watched the cars turn from the side street onto Barham Boulevard, and remembered a writer he knew from the gym, who lived someplace up there in the Hollywood Hills. He seemed like a nice guy and writers do like cats. With a hope that he will see him in the gym Andy's mood improved, and by the time he pulled into the gym's parking lot he was whistling the overture from The Merry Wives of Windsor.

As soon as he checked inn Andy snapped into his gym demeanor, blocking out the moaning and the clinking sounds of dropped weights. He moved from machine to machine without making any eye contact with the narcissistic morons, who were there to socialize. In the middle of one of his routines Andy noticed the writer's brown sport outfit, and became so anxious he dropped everything. He didn't want to look too eager so he took a deep breath, and waited for the right moment to approach him. When Andy saw the writer lift a two hundred pound weight, he tried to time himself so he can arrive when the writer drops the weight and standing up, he would see Andy's smiling face. It was not a bad idea but too theatrical and Andy tried to come up with a better one, when the writer moan. He sounded like a two hundred dollar hooker, and then he dropped the weight. The fallen steel shook the floor, and Andy was hoping the writer's moan was accidental. He watched him lift the weight again, and moan just like before. The writer flexed his muscles and was doing his circular macho walk, and when he saw Andy staring at him the writer waved. Andy waved back mumbling to himself.

"What a pompous ass."

On the end of one of his routines Andy was taking a breather when the writer came by and they politely exchanged some niceties, and then knuckle punched. They wished each other Merry Christmas, and the writer was gone when Andy realized he never mentioned him the cat.

The whole thing was a disappointment but seeing a statuesque brunette doing her floor exercise by the water fountain, Andy became very thirsty. He made a step when he noticed the long line, and watched the first guy sip some water then went back to the end of the line. Losing his thirst, Andy changed direction and headed for the treadmills.

They had four treadmills upstairs and the one on the right was available. Stepping up on the sides Andy remembered the very first time he used the contraption, and how elated he was by learning something new. Andy remembered the ease he got into the rhythm of a forced march, when somehow he lost his balance and the next thing he knew he was hanging onto the guardrails for his dear life. The incident was so vivid in his memory, it intimidated him. Andy inhaled deeply, blew air on his trigger finger and then he pushed the start button. When the running belt moved Andy stepped on, and set the speed at three miles an hour, with a raised incline. Andy used to count his steps but that was a waste of time, the treadmill was a perfect place to organize his daily chores, or to solve urgent problems like getting rid of a damned cat.

Andy looked through the large, curving windows and watched the cars swoosh by on the Hollywood Freeway. There was a slow moving cement truck crossing the bridge into Universal Studios Tours, and it reminded him the times when he was a tour guide there. Working for the Tours on his first summer vacation, Andy met Dorothy who was also a tour guide there. After their first dinner together at the Far East Terrace, he was in love with her. Two years later Andy graduated from college, got a job in the Black Tower and they got married. The two of them lived happily together for the next thirty two years. Thinking of the past everything became fresh in Andy's memory, and he recalled the day when they discussed his life without her. Dorothy joked about life does not happen very often, and she encouraged him to enjoy every remaining moments of it. Andy could never forget holding her hands as she smiled, and went to sleep. He remembered kissing her forehead, knowing that they will be together again.

Andy knew many good looking women but he would never betray Dorothy's memory, just to satisfy a cheap and overrated urge. Accepting his celibacy Andy liberated himself from the trappings of sex, and it was easy for him to stay away from the beautiful but brainless creatures. He enjoyed the simple life, loved beautiful things and was a regular visitor and member of the many museums and botanic gardens around Los Angeles. Andy had season tickets to the Hollywood Bowl, the Los Angeles Opera and the Walt Disney Concert Hall. Being physically and mentally in good shape Andy felt free, and only felt the emptiness when he stopped thinking of Dorothy. Andy watched her gentle smile appear on the screen of his memory, and then went out of focus on the huge Universal City sign.

Behind the sign where the parking structure is now there was a hill, and every year a tall Christmas tree decorated it. The tour center was small, and as they grown they needed more space. The hill was removed and was dumped into a gorge on their back lot, and when it was leveled, they moved the Colonial and Industrial streets on top of it for The Tours.

Andy remembered driving on a rainy night among a row of colorful lights, to the opening ceremony of the Sheraton Hotel. In the middle of Lou Wasserman's speech, the hillside gave way and flooded the brand new carpeted lobby with mud. Andy could never forget how pissed Lou baby was. But it was a long time ago, and Andy had urgent problems to take care of. He tried to place his mind into a problem solving mode, and placed more vigor into his steps. Andy swore he will never analyze people when he wants something from them. Moaning and dropping weights may be bad manners but it's not against the law. Who knows, the writer maybe an asshole but he could be great with cats.

Moving with a purpose Andy walked faster till he bumped into the treadmill's console and it shook him back into reality. He looked around to see if anyone noticed his blundering, but the guy on his left was off the treadmill and was talking to his friend. Since no one noticed his clumsiness, Andy relaxed and stared out the window. A motorcycle cop was writing a ticket to a driver of a BMW. The two guys must have observed the same incident because one of them said, they're all jerks.

Andy didn't know if the guy was referring to the cop or the driver of the car. He knew some BMW drivers, who drive like maniacs, but when the cop moved and Andy saw the beautiful blond behind the steering wheel, and he instantly knew she was innocent. He was wondering if the officer was a good cop or a bad cop. Andy knew there are a lot of good cops out there but most civilians don't understand the orders and the commands going down the officer's rank and file, till they get a ticket. Dealing with people is no fun, and Andy knew the police officer's job is not the happiest profession in the world.

The officer got on his bike, turned off the flash and drove away. The blond in the BMW also left and the drama came to its conclusion. Andy checked his progress, twenty minutes went by and he had no idea what to do with the damned cat. Being in a vigorous frame of mind Andy decided when he gets home he will get on the internet and learn everything about cats. He could also get on Craigslist and advertise, who knows he might make money on the one eyed cat. The thought made him snicker, and the next thing he knew he lost his balance and was hanging on to the guardrails for his dear life. A slender arm reach for the stop button, and the brunette's classic face was only inches from his, and those lips opened and asked. "Are you all right?"

Staring at her like an idiot Andy almost slipped through the guardrails, and had to gather all his strength to push up. Standing in the middle of the conveyer belt with a stupid grin on his face, Andy never felt so homesick in his entire life.

The classic faced brunette asked him again. "Are you all right?"

"I was just thinking of a cat," Andy shrugged.

The classic faced brunette's face lit up. "I love cats."

"No, the cat's not mine." Andy mumbled. "It came to my door last night."

"It rained did you let the cat in?"

"That's my problem. I don't know what to do with it?"

"Why don't you keep it?"

"Are you nuts? I'm not going to be stuck with a one eyed cat."

She stared at him for a short time but the loathsome intensity made it seem a lot longer. Andy awkwardly turned away to face her smirking entourage, and one of them was the writer. They watched him get off the treadmill walk down the steps, and out the door. Driving home Andy felt so terrible, he even wanted to forget why.

CHAPTER 3

A ndy didn't know exactly what happened but remembered calling classic face stupid. And it all started out with the cat. If the cat would not have been in his mind he would not have fallen on the treadmill, and everything would be like it was before he got the damned thing. Just by thinking of it Andy became so upset, he begin to worry about the cat's welfare. Driving home Andy decided to stop at the neighborhood Starbucks, and have his morning coffee. On Pass Avenue Andy pulled into the Vons market's parking lot, and found a parking spot near the Starbucks coffee shop. Inside Andy got a newspaper from the rack and got in line. Opening the paper he was looking for the Sports Page, when a guy bumped into him.

"I'm sorry," the guy said. "Is it always like this?"

"Yeah, it's always crowded," Andy nodded, turning away.

He knew some of the people who worked or lived in the neighborhood, and visited the place. But they also had the writers, the hustlers, and those who came to see the hustlers, so Andy liked to keep to himself. When it was his turn to order the kid scanned the newspaper, and another one went to get his coffee. After Andy paid and left a tip he headed outside, with the cup in hand and the newspaper in his armpit. He took a table on the left side of the door, and sipping his coffee Andy glanced through the pages. Reading about misguided people killing other misguided ones, Andy was relieved when he got to the sports section. The article about the Clippers was right on top, and he learned that on the end of the game the score was a tie. By doing their best the Clippers came out on top, after an intense overtime. When Andy was done reading the article he stared at the page, and knew the cat must go.

To calm down, Andy leafed to the intellectual section, and found Peanuts, by Charles M Schoulz. He was reading about Snoopy, marching on to a new adventure with the supper dish on his head. The story had its usual effect on Andy, and when he looked up the guy who bumped into him earlier was standing at his table. He asked if he can join him and Andy lost his smile, but moved the newspaper to the side.

"It's for my wife," the man said. "She'll be here in any minute."

The guy placed the paper cups on the table and Andy thought he looked familiar, but couldn't place him. Very soon a good looking blond showed up and the guy introduced her as his wife. When she said her name Andy recognized the phony southern accent, and remembered when these two were sitting at the table next to his in Big Boy's restaurant, and was pumping an old guy for his personal information. Andy remembered when they cited God's revenge if he lied, and his revulsion of the two increased.

The woman broke the silence. "Do you work for the studios?"

"I'm retired," Andy said, and watched the two of them nodding to each other.

The woman was curious. "Do you live in one of the townhouses around here?"

"No, I rent."

"Ah," the woman said with a disappointed tone.

"This way I'm not tied down," Andy explained.

"Is there a mistress?" She asked teasingly.

"No, I'd rather play the field," Andy winked, and thought it's time to turn the tide. "You two are good Christians?"

"Yes we are," they said in union.

"If you are good Christians then you must like animals?"

"Oh, we love animals," The guy responded with a reassuring smile.

"Then this is your lucky day." Andy grinned. "I have the cutest and the most beautiful kitty you have ever laid eyes on, and you can have it free."

The guy jumped from his seat. "I'm allergic to cats and I can break out just by talking about them, just look," and the guy shoved his fists under Andy's nose.

"Look for what?" Andy asked, staring at the guy's knuckles.

The guy pushed his other fists close to Andy's face, and said with an intimidating tone. "If you don't see it then you must be blind."

"Then I'm blind," Andy said standing up, and staring down at the little guy.

The hustler must have realized the party was over, because he reached for his wife and they left without a word. About twenty feet away they stopped and Andy distinctly heard him say. "Where did you find this idiot?"

"He was an easy mark, you screwed it up," the woman answered, staring at Andy.

Andy winked at her with his best smirk and she pushed her chin up, grabbing her partners arm, she pulled him away.

Clicking his pen Andy glanced after the two then turned his attention to his daily Sudoku. He was just about done when his neighbors, Jennifer and Frank Warren joined him. They wore identical tennis outfits, and were cheerful as ever.

"We drove by and saw you with that awful couple," Frank sneered, "Wanted to stop and save your ass, but couldn't find a parking space in time."

"I see you managed without us," Jennifer said, leaning on the back of a chair.

"You know those two?" Andy asked.

"We had the fortune," Frank said pulling out a chair, and seeing the coffee cops left behind by those two. "What's this?"

"It was theirs, they never touched it."

"No thanks," Jennifer said, picking up the cups and throwing them into the garbage can and then she turned to Andy. "Care to have something?"

Andy shook his head, and Jennifer went inside. They were in their forties and Andy like Jennifer's youthful vigor, and understood Frank's gaze as he looked after her. "How this two approach you?" Andy asked.

"They started out with some religious stuff," Frank recalled. "But my wife recognized the crap, and the next thing I knew she was ready to call the cops."

Andy chuckled and told them about his earlier encounter. "Now I feel guilty for not interfering, but I don't know what they do?"

"Gathering information from old people, and use it to exploit them. When they got a person's signature on the bottom of a plain paper, the game is over."

"Never sign your name on the bottom of an empty sheet of paper," Andy said.

"Amen," Frank sight then turned to Jennifer as she was coming out with cups in her hands. Andy was pleased to see how they differed and still fit so well together. Frank was a big, laid back guy, and she was like a living dynamo.

"I was telling Andy how fast you spotted our scheming friends."

Jennifer shrugged. "They pissed me off."

"Sounds like you still hold a grudge?" Andy smirked.

"I have good reasons, "Jennifer said somberly. "When I was sixteen year old a charming old couple talked me into buying their family heirloom. I never had any money so I borrowed it, and when I wanted to hock the damned thing it turned out to be a gold plated fake."

"You still have the necklace?" Andy asked.

"Yes. I keep it to remind me how gullible I was."

"I have to tell you a true story," Andy exclaimed. "I used to know this rich guy who gave fake watches to his friends on their birthdays, and I got one. One night in a garden restaurant on Melrose Avenue, I was wearing the fake Rolex, when a guy came in with a gun and took it from me. I told him to change the battery every six months, but he just stared."

"He could have killed you," Jennifer winced.

"It was a long time ago," Andy shrugged. "And now I think it was funny."

Frank turned to Jennifer. "I told you to wear it; no one will know the difference."

"But I would know it's a fake," Jennifer declared.

"It's all in your pretty head "Frank winked, stroking her hair.

Jennifer was like a little girl, when she looked at her husband. "You think I should?"

Stroking her hair frank said. "You're the only one who will know the truth."

Their lighthearted attitude made Andy realize he was tense, and glanced at his watch. "I didn't know it was so late."

Frank stretched in his chair. "It's a nice day enjoy yourself."

"It's Christmas time and I'm flooded," Andy complained.

Frank nodded. "I know what you mean, we just finished shopping."

"We were in this shopping center that was open all night long," Jennifer stated.

"I heard about them," Andy said confused, and suddenly he forgot what day it was. "When is Christmas?"

"Tonight is Christmas eve," Frank said with a curious stare.

"Are you sure?"

"Of course I'm sure," Frank said staring at Andy. "What's wrong?"

"Just lost track," Andy said. "Last night this cat came to my door, and I let it in."

"It rained and you probably saved the poor thing's life," Jennifer stated.

"I let the cat in, but I'm not sure if I saved its life?"

"You old softy," Frank said, slapping Andy's back.

Andy was thinking about hitting him twice as hard, but couldn't come up with a punch line and shrugged with a stupid grin.

"What are you going to do?" Frank asked.

"I'm trying to figure out how to get rid of the damned thing. Do you know anyone who needs a cat?"

Frank thought for a while. "How old is the cat?"

Andy showed hi palms. "It's a small thing, fits in my hand."

"Just a tiny kitty and you've already plotting against the poor thing," Jennifer stated with a sobbing tone.

Andy was surprised. "I'm not plotting; I'm trying to get rid of the damned thing."

"That's plotting."

Frank cut in. "Is it a boy or a girl?"

"I think it's a girl."

"How do you know," Jennifer snapped. "Did you look?"

"Come on guys, I just got the damned thing. I only know it scratches, eats, shits, sleeps and farts. Oh yeah, it brings bad luck."

"Is it black?" Frank asked.

"No it's gray, with a white tummy and black and white paws."

"You said it brings bad luck," Jennifer cut in.

"Since I let the damned thing in I've had nothing but bad luck."

"Then you must be superstitious," Jennifer said.

"No, I'm not."

"How do you know, did you take a test?" She asked.

"They have a test for it?"

Frank laughed. "Come on, she's pulling your leg."

"No I'm not," Jennifer declared defiantly. "He's blaming a small cat for his troubles, and I'm not going to sit here and listen to his crap."

Andy was bewildered. "What did I say to deserve this?"

Jennifer snapped again. "You're blaming a little kitty for your problems."

"Well," Andy said, scratching the back of his neck. "The damned thing created a big mess, and every time it takes a crap it stinks up the place."

"You see he admits it," Jennifer gestured.

"Cat shit smells," Andy gestured.

"What are you going to do about it?" Frank asked.

"I can't keep the cat, but I would like to place it into a decent home."

Frank deliberated. "I can ask around but most people left for the holidays,"

"Well thanks," Andy said standing up. "I hope you guys have a nice Christmas."

Frank shook Andy's hand. "Merry Christmas,"

"And stop blaming the cat." Jennifer said, clamping Andy's hand.

When Andy shook Frank's hand he asked. "Can you just keep her out of my affairs?"

"I can't, she's my watchdog," Frank said grinning at his wife, and Jennifer slapped him on the shoulder.

Watching the two Andy chuckled, and waved goodbye, "Merry Christmas."

"Consider the cat as a Christmas present." Jennifer waved, and Andy rolled his eyes.

At home Andy pulled into his parking space and turned off the engine. He opened the door and just sat there with absolutely no idea what to do with the cat. With a hope the neighbor will have some good news for him Andy got out of the car and went to his apartment.

At his door Andy was inserting the key, and wondered if he will be able to smell the cat or he was accustomed to the odor by now. But when he opened the door the sharp stanch hit him in the face. Andy went around and make sure everything was okay, and in the kitchen he picked up the empty saucer. Washing it Andy glanced at the colorful pebbles in the crap box, and wondered if he should throw them out, wash them or just let them dry. He placed the saucer on the dish rack, and watched the cat slowly stroll in the kitchen. The little thing squeaked then slowly walked to the water dish, and Andy watched it with frustration. He was an action man and liked to eliminate the problems before he could relax. But now he had no other choice but wait. Andy was thinking about getting more food for the cat just in case the neighbor will not be able to find a place for the damned cat.

Andy remembered how cold and damp the bedroom was in the morning, and he knew he can't live like this. He was ready to take a shower, and in the bathroom Andy turned on the water, adjusted the temperature and stepped under the hot stream. Soaping his body Andy was thinking about leaving the cat somewhere, but couldn't come up with a place. After he washed off the soap, Andy slowly turned off the hot water, took a deep breath and then slowly turned under the ice cold stream. When he was done Andy dried himself, and stepped on the scale. Watching the needle stop on 205 he said out loud. "Not bad for an old guy." Holding a handful of his belly flab, Andy thought if this goes he'll be as light as when he was young." And then he couldn't remember how much he weight back then.

Feeling refreshed Andy got his robe and slippers, and went to the living room to lay on the couch when the kitty presented itself with a tiny minnow. "What am I going to do with you?" Andy asked, picking up the cat.

Andy examined the bad eye and noticed it was smaller than the good one, and when he forced it open it was covered with the gray cataract.

"The eye can be fixed," Andy thought. Otherwise it was a good looking kitty, and surprisingly tame. He lifted the kitty in his left palm and the small cat just sat there, staring at him with that golden eye. The tiny thing looked helpless but Andy knew if it behaves it will survive.

Andy placed the kitty on the couch and watched it settle down. When the kitty relaxed, he stroked its back and when he tried it for the third time, the cat blocked his hand with its paws and emitted an annoyed sound. Andy believed in personal rights but a cat is a cat and he was not about to treat it like an individual. He was thinking of shoving the damned thing off the couch, but the cat looked too content. Deprived of his right to lie down Andy went in the bedroom to change into his street clothes, when he heard the doorbell ring followed by a knock on the door.

Andy rushed to see who it was and through the peep hole he saw the woman's husband from upstairs standing there. He opened the door with a cheerful smile, but the guy's somber look gave him a bad feeling and wiped the smile from his face.

"Yes?" Andy said.

"Hi Andy, it's me."

"Yes I know."

"Sorry to bother you but I wanted you to know that I made some phone calls and asked around, but unfortunately I couldn't place the cat. I will try tomorrow but I can't promise you anything, it's the holidays you know."

"I kind of figured that."

"How's the kitty?"

"The cat's fine," Andy declared. "Eats, shits, sleeps and farts. Want a smell?" Andy said opening the door, and the neighbor pushed his nose in for a sniff.

"I believe you," he said. "Well, I have to go and tell the wife I talked to you."

"Tell her to hold on to the things she finds," Andy glared.

The guy avoided Andy's stare and Andy slammed the door shut in his face, mumbling to himself. "Now I'm stuck with a one eyed cat,"

CHAPTER 4

Andy felt betrayed and helpless but in the back of his mind there was a tingle of adventure into the unknown, and the chance of learning something new. The cat appeared then stopped to groom itself and Andy was thinking of getting food for the cat. But the supermarkets are murder this time of the year, and Andy didn't feel like doing it. What the hell, I must get a bottle of wine for Sam's dinner party Andy thought, and got his jacket and picked a credit card.

The traffic on the street was ridiculous and the market's parking lot was worse. Andy followed the cars around the lot for more than half hour when a woman pushing her shopping cart crossed the road a front of him, going to her car. Andy thought he was lucky but the woman ahead of him had other ideas. She wanted him to move back so she could take the parking spot. She honked her horn and was backing into Andy's car. He looked back but there was no room to roll back to and he waited for her to hit him, but she stopped. When the cars moved ahead of her, she fallowed them showing Andy her middle finger, and he admired her Christmas spirit.

The car backed out and Andy smirked as he pulled into its parking place. When he got out and locked the doors, Andy glanced after the women's car, and wished her good luck.

Andy got a shopping cart and pushed it inside the store with aisles filled with stuff he always wanted, and if he did have it the one on the shelf looked ten times better than the one he had at home. Since you can't buy everything and you can't walk around with your eyes closed, Andy had to endure the torture and force himself to buy only the things he needed. But people like to stand around, eat the samples and block the aisles with their damned shopping carts. If someone knew what they wanted and where to get it they had no other choice but to wait, look around and buy something they don't need.

Andy had to force his way to the pet food section and looked for things the cat can use. He picked up a nice carrying case, and then he checked out a two foot red and blue, round thing with balls rolling around in grooves. First Andy thought it was for dogs, but it takes the delicate paws of a cat to hit the ball. Andy tossed it in the shopping cart, and pushing it down the aisle he got a bag of dry food, and further down the aisle he found a case of canned food. When he saw an eighty dollar scratching post, Andy thought he better move on. After he loaded the cart with some of his own needs, Andy got into the checkout lane and twenty minutes later he was driving off the parking lot, and almost an hour later he was home with more things than what he needed.

When everything was unpacked, Andy looked for the wine bottle but there was none and then he remembered standing in the checkout lane, being bothered by something he forgot. Andy took a deep breath, opened the dried food and scooped some on a plastic dish and placed it on the floor. Andy decided to have dry food out constantly, and feed the cat with canned foods in the morning. When he was done feeding the cat, Andy picked up the carrying case and went to the couch staring at the receipt. He spent over sixty dollars on the cat and he only got the damned thing. Andy unzipped the openings on the carrying case, and thought it was well made. It had a shoulder strap and the handle on top. Andy attached the straps then placed the carrying case on the floor and watched the kitty smell it. After a short examination the kitty moseyed inside and lied down. The cat did everything just right and it made Andy wonder if they can read minds. Andy heard about animals that could plot against their masters, and it made him wondered if cats were one of them. If this kitty can do more than eat, shit, sleep and fart then Andy wanted to know about it.

The cat came out of the carrying case and was playing with the straps.

"Did you stake out my place or was it a random choice," Andy said. "Admit your crime and you free to go, lie and I throw you out."

The kitty stopped playing and Andy thought the cat looked at him sideways, and then he remembered the cat has only one good eye. Andy checked his watch; it was almost seven in the evening and he didn't know where the day has gone. Changed into his t-shirt lounge pants and robe, warmed up a leftover prime rib, boiled potatoes and carrots poured himself a glass of a wine and carried them back to the couch. Andy turned on the TV and on every channel, people were celebrating Christmas. Andy stopped to watch an old rerun of Murder She Wrote, and from the floor's black and white chessboard design he recognized the abandoned Doheny Mansion's atrium, with the famous staircase from the movie; Sunset Boulevard.

When he finished his diner, Andy took the empty plates into the kitchen and washed them then refilled his wine glass and went back to the couch. Andy picked up the remote and gone through a few channels, than stopped on a black and white movie and recognized James Stuart in It's a Wonderful Life. Andy watched the bridge seen, where George Bailey wants to jump and the angel stops him. Since he already seen the movie at least a hundred times, and knew the angel will get his wings Andy he turned off the TV.

Sipping his wine he looked for the cat and if the damned thing would have read his mind, it was coming around the corner. It was the second time Andy was thinking of the kitty and it appeared and he thought the cat was reading his mind, or he was having a telepathic communication with a cat. He sent a mental message to the kitty and ordered it to stop grooming itself, but the cat kept on licking its fur. Andy concentrated his thoughts and sent a stronger mental command, but nothing happened. He tried it a few more times but he felt a headache was coming on and stopped.

"I was probably doing it all wrong," Andy mumbled, remembering the time when he was standing in the center of a treadmill and watched the brunette run on the one next to his. Even in his recollection it was hard for him to tear his eyes off of her, and when he turned he felt the burning scorn of her entourage.

Sipping his wine to ease the memory Andy stared at the cat resting on the floor and said. "I humiliated myself just by thinking of you."

The cat looked up then went back to groom its fur, and Andy knew he was blaming the kitty for his own troubles. He made a fool of himself and instead of healing his bruised ego he was blaming a cat. "Jennifer was right I'm taking my frustration out on a small cat."

Andy watched the kitty slowly walks to the couch, lifts its front paws from the floor and digs its claws into his brand new, leather couch. Not knowing what to do, Andy lifted his glass and sipped his wine, watching his brand new leather couch being destroyed by a one eyed cat he just let in the house for a night.

Andy finished his wine and felt mentally drained. He placed the empty glass on the table and adjusted the pillow, and laid his tired head on. In no time Andy dreamed that he was in a circus, standing on sawdust and wearing a lion trainer's outfit. He was holding a chair in one hand and a whip in the other, and when the music stopped and the drum rolled. The curtains opened and in a sexy outfit the classic faced brunette from the gym marched in, cranking an old Wurlitzer. The drum stopped, the Wurlitzer moaned and Andy growled, teasing the one eyed cat with the four legs of the chair. The cat scratched the air with its paws, and when Andy snapped the whip the one eyed cat jumped from one pedestal to another through a flaming loop, and then lifted its head and roared like the MGM lion.

CHAPTER 5

Andy woke up with a sore right arm, his back hurt and his neck was stiff. He remembered falling asleep on the couch and staggering into bed about two o'clock in the morning. Sitting on the side of the bed rubbing his neck, Andy swore he will never sleep on the couch again. Got his robe and coming from the bedroom he heard the shoving of the colorful pebbles, and smelled the cat. Sniffing the air Andy walked into the kitchen and tried to remember the reason he placed the shit-box in the place, where he prepares his food?

Staring at the cat, Andy was thinking about placing the shit box in the bathroom, but the place was too small. The living room and the bedroom were out of question, and Andy decided to keep it where it is and let the smell of his cooking kill the stench. The best thing would be to throw the damned cat out but it would be a death sentence, nobody in their right mind would take in a one eyed cat. There were too many unsolved problems and Andy decided to think about them during his walk in Griffith Park. He got in his hooded gym wear, and at the door he had shove the damned cat away to stop it from getting out.

On the road Andy was a bit agitated and had to watch his driving, but Errol Gardner's "Misty" calmed him down. Inside Griffith Park Andy parked his car in the Zoo's south parking lot near the fence. After he locked the car Andy pulled the hood over his head and sat his wrist watch. It was a twenty minutes stroll up to the Visitors Center, and twenty minutes back to his car. The road is about fifteen or twenty feet wide and it was built for horse-riding, but now days everybody use it. The track loops around the fenced in Harding and Wilson golf courses about two and a half miles, and the track keeps on going for another two or three miles next to the Freeway, and starts in the Equestrian Center.

Andy inhaled the fresh air as he went by the well-kept golfing greens, going in and out of the shadows of the bushes and the trees. Andy watched a flock of noisy green parrots fly above, and a squirrel was running on the top of the fence. Wildlife was everywhere and Andy imagined the one eyed cat being one of them, living off the land. Andy believed the kitty would be happy here and decided to release the cat right where he was standing. He made a few hundred steps when he heard some menacing shouts coming from the golf course. Curious to know what it was Andy stopped, and saw some golfers trying to chase a good size coyote off of their putting green. The wild creature was calmly fanned the flies off with its bushy tail, until one of the players hit it with a golf ball. The coyote got up and stared at the golfer, and then calmly wandered away. The coyote crawled under the fence and Andy watch the well fed beast cross the road affront of him, and immediately realized the one eyed cat would not be happy here.

Watching the coyote Andy remembered reading a newspaper article about cougars living in the Santa Monica Mountains, and the one named P22 was roaming the Los Feliz area. "I must be going nuts," Andy mumbled, and watched a young couple speed up as they went by.

Coming up with stupid ideas really bothered him, and now he was afraid to think and come up with something that would hurt the cat. When Andy reached the road where it curves around the golf course, he walked up to the railing and spit in the direction of the Visitor's Center. He actually liked the place and used their spotless facilities many times. Andy just liked to mark the halfway point by spitting over the railings.

Turning around Andy checked the time; he covered the first mile in twenty minutes. On his way back he stopped at the place where the wood fence on the roadside was just the right height and done twenty-four pushups on it, one for every hour of the day. He was glad to count since it was impossible to say the numbers, and come up with something brilliant that would harm the cat.

Widely circling with his arms Andy inhaled and watched the civilized game of golf amid nature's brutal struggles he would have never noticed if it was not for the cat. On his way back to the car Andy left the track and followed the main road to reach the parking lot. The path went through a grassy patch, where he rubbed the bottom of his shoes on to the grass to brush the dirt from the grooves. When Andy reached the parking lot, he stomped his foot onto the asphalt to remove the remaining dirt from his shoes. When he was done his mind was free again, and the damned cat popped in his mind. Just the thought of leaving a tamed animal out in the wild made Andy sick, and by the time he got to his car he had to inhale twenty four times before he was able to open the car's door.

"Nothing happened," Andy mumbled. 'I was only thinking of leaving the damned cat out her in the wild." But pulling the safety belt over his chest, his conscience bothered him. The only reason Andy was so successful at Universal Studios, because he always made his decisions based on valid information and not on his impulses. Andy was always better prepared than the opposition, and after he persuade them to accept his ideas he would please them with bullshit. For the first time in his adult life Andy made a decision without any information to back it up, and it really hurt his pride. Holding his breath Andy counted up to twenty four before he started the engine, and to forget his mental blunder, Andy pushed the player button on the CD. The speakers blurted Lehar's melody from The Land of Smiles, and the schmaltz made him remember his father's altered quotation of Nietzsche: "If it doesn't kill you it will turn you into a superman."

The concept cheered him up and Andy was singing the love song along with Mario Lanza, knowing he would be a good singer if he had a voice for it. Walking on the dirt in Griffith Park and now driving on a paved road, Andy was able to see the way civilization asphalted itself into nature to create its own trappings. Andy was an Angelino and saw Los Angeles spread over the orange groves. The atmosphere of an evolving city is always filled with new ideas, and Andy considered himself a modern man. He was also a God fearing man who questioned the creation theory, and came to believe that evolution was God's way of turning a creature into a man. Andy also believed, when humans learned to dominate the other species they also became responsible for the health and welfare of the planet. And now he is responsible of the goddamned cat.

Turning on to his street Andy stopped for a squirrel and honked the horn. The squirrel rushed to the sidewalk to hide behind a tree. Andy was a careful driver but this time he stopped for the squirrel out of understanding, and it made him feel good.

At home Andy parked his car, and going to his apartment he was thinking about being acclimated to the stench, but when he opened the door it hit him right in the face. He was looking for the damned thing but it had a tendency to know when to hide.

After his breakfast Andy saw some cat hairs fly around, and it made him wonder how many of them have he swallowed. "I must get rid of the damned cat before it changes my DNA," Andy grumbled. He decided to mention the cat to Sam, and hoped he will give him some good advice. They were good friends now, but there was a time when Andy thought that Sam was a forceful black man, who hacked his way into his all white neighborhood with his sports money. Andy didn't mind seeing Sam in a game, but having him as a neighbor in his all white district was out of the question. His feelings were well documented in the articles he wrote in the local news-paper, proving what an old fashioned bigot Andy really was. But despite of Andy's efforts, Sam bought the place.

Andy's dislike of Sam went on, till a Fourth of July firecracker changed everything. It was almost twenty three years ago when they were able to see the Fourth of July fireworks in the Rose Bowl from his backyard, and they had some friends over to watch the fireworks. Everybody was comfy in their lunge chairs facing north-east, when some idiot close to Huntington Drive sent up a rocket and it swooshed over them and landed just about where Sam's house was. Andy heard the pop, and saw the black smoke rising. He rushed in the house and called 911, and then he went outside were Dottie was waiting for him with the golf cart and they drove to Sam's house. As soon as they turned the corner they saw a burning tree next to an open window with a balcony. Andy jumped off the cart and climb up to the window, and Dorothy drove to the main door. By the time

Andy got over the railings the curtains in the window cut fire and he rushed over to rip them off, waking up the woman inside.

"What are you doing in here?" The woman said getting out of bed, and Andy recognized Dolores, Sam's pregnant wife.

"You must get out of here, the tree is on fire," Andy said, stamping on the burning curtains on the ground.

Dolores looked around the now smoke filled room, and saw the flames leaping through the window. The bedroom door opened and Dorothy came with some help, and they escorted Dolores to safety. When the fire trucks arrived the fireman extinguished the flames, with some water damage to the bedroom.

Andy and Dorothy were glad Dolores was safe, and watched her ordering the help to serve coffee and sandwiches to the fireman. In the process Dolores gone into labor and was taken to the hospital. Later in the day Andy and Dorothy visited her in the hospital, and they were present when she gave birth to a son. The next day when Sam came home he found them asleep in their chairs, next to his wife's bed.

It was the beginning of a friendship between Dolores and Dorothy, and it spread over to Sam and Andy, with little Raymond running between the two households. Afraid of having another fire Sam tore down the old wood building and replaced it with a marble one. It reminded Andy of Swiss cheese with warm holes, and just hated place.

Placing the Christmas presents into his car's trunk, Andy was thinking about the choices he made since Dorothy past away, and everyone was the wrong one. He sold his ancestral home in San Marino, and now lives in an apartment with a one eyed cat.

Andy readjusted the packages so he can close the trunk, and went back to his apartment to change. Being a holiday and all,

Andy picked a sport coat with a necktie. No one wears a top coat in Southern California, but the nights can be chilly, and Andy shoved a red cashmere scarf into his jacket's pocket. He was brushing the dust from his shoes when he heard a scratching sound, and saw the kitty sink its nails into his brand new leather couch. In every normal situation Andy would have thrown the brush at the cat with intend to kill, but he just watched the one eyed cat giving his new couch a worn look. Andy cringed as he went by, and didn't even bother to push the kitty away. In the kitchen Andy took a cheap bottle of vine from the rack and read the label when the kitty stroll in and set on the floor by the shit box, glaring at him with that eye,

"After my leather couch there's nothing worthy for your nails in here," Andy asserted, filling the anger building. "I've bought your stuff and forgot to buy the wine. Now I have to take this crap to the party." Andy said, grabbing the bottle by the neck and threatening the cat with it. The cat jumped and ran away, and then stopped outside the kitchen looking confused. Andy saw a red Macy's bag with the handles by the trashcan, and placed the wine bottle inside. He refilled the cat's drinking water, scooped some more dry food into the dish and checked for things that could harm the cat. Finding everything in order Andy took the scarf from his pocket, wrapped it around his neck, and wished the damned cat a Merry Christmas. He was ready to leave when he remembered the wine, and went back to get the Macy's bag.

CHAPTER 6

When Andy entered the Freeway he heard something was rolling around but didn't know what it was, and was hoping it was not the car. When he changed into the fast lane he heard the noise again, and when he looked back he saw the round toy with the balls rolling in the grooves. Andy reached back to shove the toy from the seat to the ground, and when he turned back the traffic ahead of him slowed to a stop, and he was still going sixty miles an hour. Andy pushed the brakes and stopped only inches from the car ahead him, but the cars behind him did not. After the first car hit him he heard the tires screeching, and winced every time a car crashed into another one. Andy pulled to the embankment, and when he stepped out of the car he saw a row of wrecks. The drivers were standing by their cars with cellphones to their ears, and they all stared at him.

A motorcycle officer showed up and placed out flares, and when he went by Andy wanted to talk to him, but the officer hold up his hand and asked. "Are you hurt?"

Andy rubbed the back of his neck. "My neck is stiff but yes, I'm okay."

"Good," the motorcycle cop said, and went on to do his work. Some more police arrived, and the motorcycle cop explained to them what he observed so far, and vent back to Andy.

"Is everyone's okay?" Andy asked.

The cop nodded. "Everyone seems to be fine."

"It's hard to believe that all those cars just ran into each other," Andy exclaimed.

"Cars tend to follow one another," the police explained.

But Andy was incredulous. "How could six cars run into each other?"

"There are seven cars involved," the policeman said, staring at the damaged cars.

"You mean I was the seventh?"

"You were the first, and those people back there are blaming you. Do you have a valid California driver's license?" The cop asked.

Andy took out his wallet, removed his driver's license and handed it to the officer. Glancing at the license the cop went back to his motorcycle and got on the radio. When the cop came back he stared at Andy like a cat would observe a canary, and handed back Andy driver's license.

"Tell me what happened?" The officer asked, and his eyes didn't blink.

Andy told him that he was going about sixty miles an hour when suddenly the cars slowed down, and stopped.

"Have you been drinking?"

"No, but hopefully I will have a glass of wine with my dinner," Andy smiled.

The officer took out his flashlight and directed the beam into Andy's eyes. "Watch my finger, "the policeman said, holding up his index finger and was examining Andy's pupils. After the officer was done with Andy, he directed his flashlight's beam into the car. The beam went over the Macy's bag with the wine, and stopped on the round toy. Andy was sure the cop can figure out what happened and was ready to confess, when the policeman turned and asked. "Do you have a cat?"

Andy was surprised. "How do you know?"

"My cats have one of those," the officer said pointing to the round toy with such a friendly smile Andy thought he was a real human being.

After the cop's cordial demeanor vanished, Andy had to prove the car was his and had proper car insurance. When the cop was done, he introduced Andy to the guy who hit his car, and wished them Marry Christmas.

Andy exchanged information with the guy, and on the end they wished each other Merry Christmas. Andy was finally able to call Sam's house and told his wife Dolores that he was in an accident, and will be late. Waiting for the tow truck Andy also got in touch with his insurance agent, and the lady on the phone was very nice. She wanted to know if he was hurt and did he wore a seatbelt or had a drink. The insurance lady suggested a car repair shop, and then she wished him Mary Christmas. Andy had nothing else to do but wait for the tow-truck, and stare at the damaged car trunk with the Christmas presents inside. As his frustration grew Andy was thinking up ways to get rid of the cat but they were too gruesome, and he had to tone it down to choking the damned cat to death with his bare hands. When Andy realized his ghastly intents, he mumbled to himself in horror.

"My good God what am I thinking, it's Christmas day."

CHAPTER 7

By the time the taxi arrived at Sam's gate it was close to ten o'clock at night, and the party was over. But Andy was tired, stubborn and needed a stiff drink. He got out of the car and pushed the button on the intercom, and told them he was outside. When the gates opened they drove in, and drove on the moonlighted, gravel road. Bushes, trees and flowers surrounded the path, and they got to a circular driveway with a fountain in the center. They stopped in front of a marble mansion, and Andy paid the cab.

When Andy turned, he saw Sam's wife Dolores waiting for him in the ornate doorway of a marble mansion. She was a tall and sexy, middle aged Latina.

"I haven't seen you in ages. I heard you were in an accident."

"I'm okay," Andy said, fake kissing her. "The presents are in the car's trunk."

"Don't worry about them, the main thing's you're not hurt. Now everyone's gone and I'm with my friends."

Andy followed her through the marble corridor into a sunken living room, where Dolores introduced Andy to her friends. One was the wife of a famous quarter back, and the other woman was the wife of a receiver.

Andy inquired where their husbands were and was told they let them go so they can enjoy a decent conversation, without having any man around. Andy got the hint asked were Sam was, and Dolores pointed to the back. He handed her the Macy's bag. "This is the nectar of the Gods," and Andy left.

One of her friends asked Dolores. "What's that?"

"It's some cheap wine," Dolores said, throwing the Macy's bag with the wine in the trashcan, then joined her friends and lifted her wine glass. "He probably never tasted Petrus Pamerol."

Andy heard the sarcastic laughter as he walked through the marble corridors, but was too involved with hating the place. Andy felt like being in a Swiss cheese, with worm holes. He opened the back door and stepped into a lush garden with a huge, natural stone swimming pool surrounded by a wooden sundeck, with lunge chairs, and Andy inhaled. There were some bungalows by the fence, and Andy approached one of them. When he opened the door Andy fanned his hands. "This place is like the den of iniquity."

"Just look who the wind blew in," Sam said getting out of his chair. He was a huge black man in his mid-fifties, with a friendly smile. Sam was still in good shape but the good life was beginning to show around his waist. They shook hands, and Sam had to bend from his six foot seven inch height to rub shoulders with Andy.

"Merry Christmas bro, long time no see," Sam said.

"Good seeing you Sam, Merry Christmas."

"I heard you were in an accident, are you all right?" Sam asked, going back to his chair.

"I have a sore neck, but I'll be alright."

"A whiplash is not a joke."

"Yes it is, just ask any lawyer."

Sam shook his head and laughed. "Every bump leaves a mark. Sometimes I'm sore in places I never knew I had them."

"I believe you. Where's Raymond?"

"They left. Get yourself a drink, or you want one of this?" Sam said, opening an elegant humidor case and removed a joint.

"I stick with my old poison, if you don't mind. Do you want me to fix you anything?" Andy asked, walking up to the well-stocked bar

"No thanks," Sam said, feeding his Chromium crusher with buds.

Andy walked behind the bar and filled a water glass with scotch, and enjoying it almost naked, he splashed it with water. Lifting his glass Andy felt his neck hurt, and rubbing it he turned his head left and right.

"You right, I think I go and see a doctor."

"No, you see a lawyer first and then they will refer you to a chiropractor," Sam explained.

Andy was indignant. "I don't want to make any money out of it."

"Why not, it's free?" Sam was lighting the crushed buds in his glass bong.

"I can't suit my soul and my pocketbook in the same time," Andy theorized.

"You used to tell me I was wasteful, and just look at you," Sam exclaimed.

"I also told you to be honest," Andy said, sipping his Scotch.

"You told me that your neck hurts, are you lying to me?" Sam asked.

"Okay, let me think about it," Andy said.

"That's all you have to do," Sam clarified.

Andy was rubbing his neck. "I'm an active person, I ski Mammoth, I play tennis and I never got hurt."

"You never fall on a ski slope?" Sam asked.

"I got bruised, but so far I've gone through life without any major injuries."

Sam was watching Andy taste his drink, and carry it back to his chair. "Bruises never bothered me; it's the career ending injury that I was afraid of. And you can't even think about it."

"What do you mean can't you think?" Andy asked.

Sam stared into the air. "If you do, it always happens."

Andy was incredulous. "How you cope with that?"

"You don't think, just do," Sam uttered.

"How can you not think when every sport is a mental game?" Andy asked.

Sam was thinking for a moment. "It's mental for the coaches on the sidelines. Players practice till every move is instinctual."

"Action and reaction like a robot," Andy said.

"They would like you to be one," Sam said, emptying the bong and filling it with freshly ground marihuana buds.

"I don't think I could put up with that," Andy exclaimed, sipping his drink.

"You're privileged and never had to. There are kids out there whose only hope is to make it in sports. If they fail their life is ruined."

"My life wasn't that easy."

"But it was secured from the beginning," Sam took a drag and stared in the air. "In sports only the best survives."

Andy gulped his Scotch. "I believe you."

"Are you sure you don't want one of this?" Sam asked, showing Andy a joint.

"No thanks," Andy said, finishing his drink and stood up to make another stiff one. He was in a mood to get drunk.

"So you didn't want Raymond to be hurt?" Andy asked, placing his glass on the bar and lifting the bottle of scotch.

Sam was incredulous. "What do you mean by that?"

"You let him quit basketball," Andy stated.

Sam was staring at Andy. "No I did not. I think somebody talked him out of it?"

"That son of a bitch," Andy said, filling his glass.

"That's what I said," Sam muttered, taking a drag and not taking his eyes off of Andy.

"What a shame, Raymond is so good."

"Don't forget he's six foot nine."

"Six foot nine and we lost him to science?" Andy nodded, then sipping his scotch he walked back to his chair.

Sam stared in the air. "I think stupidity runs in my family."

"What a waste," Andy said sitting down.

"Yeah, no one in my family was ever in a thinking business, we all did something for a living; I think he got it from his mother."

"But at least he's a scientist."

Sam puffed on his pipe and was holding his breath until he turned purple, and then blew a perfect O ring. "You know me I'm always eye to eye, but Ray's friends think they know everything. They talk down to people, and I don't like that."

"Sam, Raymond is a scientist and speaks a different language."

"That's what I'm talking about, the language. They all sound like women."

Now Andy was interested. "Are you kidding me?"

"I don't mind if my wife comes up with some crazy stuff," Sam explained. "But when my son thinks like a woman that hurts."

Andy guzzled his drink. "Holly shit, have you tried to talk him out of it?"

"It's no use."

"But you still love him, don't you?"

"Of course, he's my son."

"Then accept him the way he is."

"Believe me I'm trying but it's not easy," Sam said, puffing on his pipe.

"You handle it so well. How come I never noticed it?"

Sam held his breath than exhaled the smoke. "I just want to save him from the bad things I went through, but it's useless. They think they know everything."

"The main thing is you love him, and he knows he can depend on you," Andy said, emptying his glass.

"I blame myself for being away, and not spending enough time with him."

"But what could you have done, they're born that way?"

Sam glared at Andy. "What the hell are you talking about?"

"You told me he's gay."

"When have I told you that?"

"You just said that he and his friends are talking like women."

"You must be hearing things, he's getting married. I hope it will be soon or she won't fit into her wedding dress."

"You mean she's pregnant?"

Sam nodded.

"That's beautiful you're going to be a grandpa. Congratulations," Andy said with his outstretched hand and was trying to get up. Sam shoved his palm in the air, to stop him.

"Sit down; I don't want you to get hurt."

"I'm just happy for you," Andy said, sinking back into his chair.

Sam stared at Andy and said. "I know."

"Then what are you bitching about?"

"He is an atheist."

"He's an atheist? " Andy jumped from his chair. "Did you try talking him out of it?"

"I don't think you can."

Andy staggered to the bar, leaned on it and pointed upward. "Only those who believes in him shall be saved,"

"You're his godfather, why don't you tell him that?" Sam stated.

"I will," Andy said, looking for his glass.

Sam watched him staggered back for it. "I have never seen you drunk."

Andy picked up the glass and carefully zigzagged back to the bar. "I've never had a reason for it, "Andy said filing his glass.

"The accident really got to you."

Andy sprinkled his scotch with water. "It's not the accident, but if I would tell you, you won't believe me."

"Try me."

"I was watching the Clippers game," Andy said drying his hand with a towel.

"I saw it too. DJ rebound like never before, JJ made all his three pointers, and Chris was great. I think Griffin had at least twenty six points?" Sam explained. "The Timberwolves played their hearts out, and only lost in overtime."

Andy became furious. "When I get home I'm going to kill the cat."

"I didn't know you have a cat?"

"I told you I watched the game," Andy leaned on the bar, sipping his drink. He told Sam about the cat, and the stupid things he have done. In the dark corner of the room Sam snickered with tears in his eyes, and when Andy finished telling the story Sam burst into a body shaking laughter.

Andy woke up with a terrible hangover, and a stiff neck. It took him some time to realize he was in Sam's bungalow, and went to wash his face. When Andy recognized himself in the mirror, he threw up. With shaking hands Andy tore some toilet paper from the roll, and wiped the places he hit when he missed the bowl. After Andy cleaned everything he washed his face again, and examined himself in the mirror. The bloodshot eyes and the messed up hair made him shudder, and with shaking hands Andy re buttoned his now wrinkled shirt. When he came out of the bathroom he looked for the rest of his clothes, and found his shoes but only one of the sacks. He pulled it on his left foot and got his shoes on, when Sam walked in wearing white tennis shirt, and shorts. Sam was holding a tennis racket, and looked so healthy it was sickening.

"Are you ready for a few rounds?" Sam asked, tapping the tennis racket into his left palm.

"No thanks," Andy said and went in the kitchen to get a glass of water. When the cold water hit his now empty stomach it made him sick and Andy run back in the bathroom. Hearing the sickening noise coming from the toilette, Sam chuckled and shook his head. When Andy came out he was shaking and sweating.

"I guess not," Sam said. "We've left you a package in the kitchen, it's a turkey lag. There are taxi cab numbers next to the phone, and don't be a stranger," Sam said, hugging Andy by the shoulder. "You're family," Sam said, wiping his hand in the back of his pants. At the doorway Sam stopped and came back. "I should give you a few of this," Sam said, taking a pack of cigarette from his pocket.

Andy was in shock. "I didn't know you smoked?"

"No I don't. I just want you to have this," Sam said, and took three joints from the pack.

"I really don't want them," Andy said pushing Sam's hand away, but Sam placed them in his shirt pocket.

"You can always throw them away, but believe me it's the best thing to cure a hangover."

Shaking and sweating, Andy got in a chair and when he looked up Sam was walking out the door. The first thing he wanted to do is to get home and take a shower. Andy put on his jacket and was looking for his necktie, and found it hanging on the door knob. Andy looked for his other sock but gave up and walked out of the place.

Going to the kitchen at the back of the marble mansion, Andy heard the sound of tennis balls, and with his hangover it was hard to believe that people could do those things so early in the morning. In the kitchen Andy found the note with a taxi cab number, and called one. There was also a package, and when Andy looked in he saw soup in a container, and a turkey lag. With the package in hand Andy rushed through the marble corridors, and when he stepped outside the sun almost blinded him. He rushed to an old fashioned park bench under a bushy tree, and laid down on it. In no time Andy was asleep, and was awakened by somebody shaking him. Andy looked up and saw the taxi cab driver, and he hit his hands away. Andy stared at him with his bloodshot eyes, and then stood up and adjusted his necktie. He pulled on the collar of his now wrinkled shirt, adjusted his necktie, and then picked up his package. Andy walked to the cab and waited for the driver to open the door, but he was already behind the steering wheel. Andy told the driver the address, got in the cab. He leaned back and the movement of the car almost made him sick, but the pleasant sound of the gravel under the tires calmed him down. There was another car approached them, it was a limousine with the windows down and Andy recognized Jerry West, Magic Johnson, and Shaquille O'Neal, and it made Andy wonder why would they come to visit visiting Sam?" When they turned on the freeway ramp Andy was wondering if he would be able to recognize the scene of the accident, and when they drove by the glass shards glittered in the sun, and the taxi driver narrated. "There was an accident here last night. Six cars ran into each other."

"It was a seven car pileup," Andy stated.

The driver was curious. "How do you know?"

"I read it in the newspaper," Andy lied.

"I thought the papers were late this morning."

"I read it in the New York Times."

The driver was astounded. "It's already in the New York Times?"

"Yes, in the western edition."

"Ah!" The driver said, checking out Andy in his rearview mirror.

When they arrived Andy paid for the ride, and the cab driver watched him walk away in his wrinkled clothes with one missing sock, and murmured. "New York Times my ass."

CHAPTER 8

At his apartment's door Andy reached into his right pocket for the house keys, and they were not there. His heart was racing when he remembered waking up in the middle of the night, and removing the keys from his pocket because it was tearing into his leg. Andy reached into his left pocket and was relieved when he felt the keys.

"I should keep them together with the car keys," Andy said, and tried to remember why he separated them.

Sick with hangover Andy inhaled like a fish takes in water, and held his breath. He exhaled and with his shaking hand he found the hole in the lock and turned the key. He jubilantly opened the door, when the cat's odor hit him in the face. Andy just wanted to take a shower and rest, when he remembered to feed the cat. As soon as Andy was in his robe, he went in the kitchen where he opened a can of cat food, and poured it all in the dish. He wanted the cat to have enough food, just in case he goes to bed and sleeps for the next two or three days. The cat must have heard the sound of the can opening, because it appeared and Andy watched the kitty band over the dish. "How can a small thing create all that problems, just by doing nothing?"

Andy was in no shape to figure things out, and became so eager to be clean he even enjoyed turning the shower knobs. Andy skipped the cold splash knowing it would kill him, and just enjoyed a nice worm spray. When Andy was done he felt slightly better, and a lot cleaner.

In the kitchen Andy opened the package and removed the chicken soup in a Styrofoam bowl, covered with a plastic lid. He also checked the turkey leg with all the trimmings, in a Styrofoam tray. Andy poured the soup into a porcelain bowl and placed it into the microwave oven. Not trusting the seals to hold the radiation inside, Andy left the kitchen. At his desk he checked his E-mails and was almost done when the oven signaled. He went back in the kitchen and with safety gloves on, Andy removed his soup from the microwave. Being a good Christian man Andy always said a few words of prayer before he ate but this time he said the hell with it. Andy lunged at the bowl and the soup was so delicious, he picked up the dish with a few spoonful of soup left in it, and slurped it. Wiping his mouth with the sleeve of his house coat, Andy sniffed and looked out the window. It was a beautiful clear day, and he felt slightly better but not good enough to enjoy it. To get things out of the way Andy washed the dish and then headed to the bedroom, got in bed, and before his head hit the pillow he was asleep.

Andy woke up with a headache and didn't know if it was morning, noon or night. Andy just laid there till he remembered the accident, and getting drunk at Sam's house. The knot in his stomach became tighter and Andy had to go to the toilet, but held it back. When Andy finally got out of bed he got his robe and slippers on, and set back on the bed. He tried not to think or make any sudden moves, and remained there till nature forced him to move.

Walking around must have done him good because in the bedroom Andy adjusted the bed cover, emptied his pants pocket and threw the change in the jar. He was about to throw his white shirt in the laundry basket when he remembered Sam's presents, and removed them from his shirt pocket. Andy went in the kitchen, turned on the fan and found a lighter. Got in his chair and rolled the joint between his fingers, noticing the filter. Andy remembered smoking filtered Marlboro, when he was young and stupid.

Andy lit the joint, and for the first time since his college days he enjoyed its fragrance. Andy held his breath when the kitty walked in, set by the shit box and stared at Andy with that eye. "Are you spying on me?" Andy said, filling guilty for being cut by a cat smoking weed. Blowing the smoke out Andy realized that Sam was right, he still had a hangover but there was a difference. The cat was staring at him and Andy growled. "What are you looking at I suppose to kill all nine of your lives. I'm just not in the mood for a massacre."

Andy placed the joint on the sink and stood up to pour some more dry food out for the cat. He refilled the water dish and stroked the kitty. Andy lit up the joint again and watched the cat, knowing the damned thing didn't do anything wrong. He was the one who overacted out of sheer incompetence. "It was my own stupidity," Andy admitted. "You can't fake knowledge."

Andy toke another dreg and held his breath like Sam, and tried to blow an O ring. He tapped the side of his face, but only puffs of smoke came out. Andy was holding his nose twisted his finger in one ear and looked cross eyed but he couldn't puff an O ring, and the cat was watching his every move.

"You think it's funny?" Andy asked, and the kitty got closer. "We are nuts," Andy pointed to himself. "You see kitty, we humans always do something stupid, and that's how we learn. A day can be wasted if don't do something wrong, do I make any sense to you?"

Holding the finished joint by the filter Andy went to the sink and held it under the running water before he dumped it in the trash. The effect of the cannabis must have cut up with him because he was still sick, but in a good mood. Andy heated water and made tea without the rum. He placed his tea mug on the kitchen table, and pushed the two remaining joints aside. Sipping his tea Andy turned to the cat. "Well, where were we?"

Andy remembered hating school, even though it was the only place where they teach you something, and you don't have to do anything stupid for it. "You see kitty nothing comes to us naturally. We don't even know that we are mammals, trying to be human." Andy said, watching the kitty, grooming itself. "You see kitty being half beasts and half human, the side we choose is what we are."

Andy was thinking about what he just said but it was too complicated. He picked up his tea mug, sipped the brew and stared at the cat. "How come you're a cat, did you choose to be one?" Andy asked, finishing his tea.

He stood up to make another cup when his stomach growled, and found himself stoned and hungry. Andy removed the turkey diner from the fridge, and piled everything on a plate. He placed the dish in the microwave oven, and picked up the cat before he pushed the start button. Stroking the kitty Andy went in the living room and placed the small thing on the back of the couch. He leaned over, facing the kitty. "The only people you've ever known throw you out, and with all the doors in the city you wound-up at mine."

Staring at the helpless thing Andy's sympathy grow, and was ready to help the cat but didn't know how. "We all try to survive, but you can't stay here," Andy said, stroking the small cat. "After the holydays we'll found a doctor to fix that eye, and hopefully I will get rid of you."

The kitty pressed its head against Andy's stroking hand, and when he rubbed its neck the cat just melted on the top of the couch. The microwave signaled and Andy left the cat on the top of the couch, and went back in the kitchen. With mittens on Andy removed the hot plate from the oven, and placed it on the kitchen table. The diner was so delicious Andy licked the bone and he thrown it on the floor. The kitty struggled with the large turkey bone, and Andy wondered how the small cat got to it from the top of the couch.

When Andy was finished eating he wiped his mouth in the sleeve of his robe, and sniffed. Staring out the kitchen window Andy saw the twilight, and not seeing the squirrels around the crooked tree, he had a weird sensation of being lost in time. Andy went to the sink, washed the dishes and then made tea with rum, lemon and honey. Sipping his brew by the kitchen table Andy watched the small cat struggle with the turkey bone.

"Hey kitty, there was a turkey walking on that bone. You see kitty we humans do like the other species baked or fried." Andy knew the cat doesn't understand a word, but he was stoned and couldn't stop thinking. "I want you to listen and listen well," Andy said to the cat seating affront of him, and staring at him with that eye. "You can't trust humans because we consume the other species to survive. I can bet you there's a guy out there who would love to have you for diner."

The kitty closed the eye, and Andy thought the cat understood what he just said. "You see Kitty we are predators. We eat, shit and sleep just like you do, and only our ability to reason we are human. Being half human and half beasts, the side we choose is what we are. When we are beasts, we spend more money on weapons then on food, and it's hard for me to understand why an innocent kitty like you would ever want to be near a human being?"

Andy picked up the rum bottle and enriched his tea. "We call it the dog's hair," Andy mumbled, showing the bottle to the cat. The drink didn't taste the way he thought it would but Andy finished it anyway, and staring at the empty tea mug he felt worn out. Andy stroked the kitty then went to the bedroom and back to bed.

CHAPTER 9

The holydays were gone and armed with what he learned about cats Andy was looking forward to 2013. Seating at the kitchen table by the window, Andy watched the kitty play with a new toy. He was thinking about taking the cat to a doctor and let them look at that eye. On the internet he found a clinic nearby and wrote down the address. When he dialed the number a tired voice answered, and Andy made an appointment for the following day. He never been inside an animal clinic and imagined it will be like the ones he visits, but working with animals they probably wear blue jeans. It's also an easier job because the patients don't talk back.

Andy appreciated good doctors. He found out that not many of them have the dedication of an Albert Schweitzer. Most of them became doctors because their parents urge them to be one, and they are all in for the money. Some doctors loath their patients, and most of them think they are smarter than the sick ones. When you must see a doctor it's like placing yourself into God's hands, because they can put you there. Andy learned that walking into a doctor's office is a gamble, you'll never know if you're going to meet Doctor Jackal or Mr. Hyde. No matter which one you're going to see you have to give them respect, because sooner or later they will enter your body at every opening. And in places they can't enter they cut their way in. They treat you like a piece of biff and think of you as a money making meat, but despite all of that they have your respect. There was a time when Andy became so paranoid, at night before he went to sleep; he counted people in white coats jump over him and not sheep.

The noise from the garbage truck shook him back into reality, and saw the squirrels stopped chasing each other around the crooked tree. They watched the noisy monster lift the blue bin, and emptying it into its belly. Andy heard a squeak and when he looked down the kitty was there, staring at him. Andy picked up the tiny thing and placed it on the books to look out the window. When the cat saw the squirrels it crouched, and lowered its head. Andy was standing there and the squirrels never paid attention to him, but seeing the small cat they stopped playing, and now the three of them were staring at each other.

It was interesting to see how the primitive survival instincts turned the small cat into an arched backed hunter, ready to pounce and kill. Andy didn't think the kitty knew that squirrels crack nutshells with their teeth, it was only aware of its own impulses. We may experience something similar when we are cold and hungry, and pass another person on a dark street.

The kitty tensed and its head shifted with short searching moves, and without looking out the window Andy knew the squirrels were gone. His own understanding of the cat's primitive instincts was a surprise to him, since he considered himself a civilized person. He was born and raised in Los Angeles, and went to USC film school. He put together great motion pictures and TV shows, but he never was around animals.

But without animals Andy had more time for other things, and with Dorothy they traveled the world. They met all kinds of interesting people, and learned the struggle to survive was the same everywhere. Everything they saw and experienced was educational and their respectful interest in other people's faith helped their own spiritual growth. Visiting all the five populated continents, the different cultures fascinated them. They noticed how willingly people submitted themselves to the prevailing order, as long as they were free to practice whatever they believed in. Andy had great discussions with Dorothy about the influence of faiths, and the power the leaders have over the believers. Andy trusted the separation of church and state here in the United States because it allowed American Democracy to evolve and grow, and flood the world with the products of the free and open mind.

But Dottie only saw the good in everybody, and was intelligent enough to respect whatever they believed in. With Dottie, Andy discussed everything, and one of their most interesting debates was about Hitler's Nazi Germany. Dorothy believed that Hitler was an evil genius who manipulated the German people. And Andy placed Hitler in the same group with Idi Amin, Poll Pot and Jim Jones, of the Jonestown fame, only worse.

Remembering their intellectual debates Andy couldn't help but smile, when something scared the cat and jumped off the books. Andy wasn't even back into reality, when he stopped the small cat jumping off the table. Holding the kitty up, it sunk its claws into Andy's shoulder and he was surprised to see how easily she was frightened. Andy gently placed Cilla on the floor and stroked it. "You sure have claws." Andy said, rubbing his shoulder.

Andy looked out the window but not seeing anything that could have frighten him, Andy turned and his eyes stopped on a small drawer. He went there and pulled it out, finding inside two of Sam's pre-rolled gifts. Andy removed one with a Bic lighter and went back to the kitchen. He turned on the fan and lighted the joint, watching a noisy crow fly on the top of the crooked tree. The crow bitched for a while then flew away. Andy inhaled and his eyes wondered to the framed picture of Dorothy on his desk. He picked it up and stared at her, holding on to a tram's handle bar, with one shapely leg on the tram's step. Andy remembered being very chummy with her at Mark's house party, when Mark was still a tour guide and not the manager of the Universal Amphitheatre.

Andy admired Dorothy's statuesque form but she was too chummy with a tour guide named Michael Ovitz, and Andy considered her off limits. To Andy's surprise she was very friendly at Mark's party, and after they smoked a joint they walked out to the tennis court and made love on a bench. Thinking of it Andy chuckled, because it was not even love at first sight.

Andy found Dorothy too easy and tried to avoid her, but one day at the paycheck window Dorothy came out of nowhere, and Andy couldn't escape. He had the tendency to face trouble head on, so after he got his weekly check, Andy walked up to Dorothy and grabbed her by the waist. When he kissed her on the cheek she pushed him away, and Andy was surprised. Not knowing what to do he was about to walk away, but Dorothy faced him.

"What's going on, are you hiding from me?"

Her voice was ringing in Andy's ears if she would have been standing there right now, and remembered when he. "I'm sorry I was studying for exam."

Andy can never forget the look on her face, and it made him feel guilty. To show his sincerity Andy invited Dorothy to diner at the

Far East Terrace, and that night Dottie whipped Andy off his feet, and decided to spend the rest of his life with her. Andy never learned that man doesn't choose their woman. It's the other way around. The party at Mark's house was a setup to bring the two of them together, because Dorothy was already in love with him.

It reminded Andy of his father's warnings, that you can live your life and plan your days and someone, somewhere already changed it for you,"

CHAPTER 10

When Andy was ready to take the cat to the doctor he opened the carrying case and placed it on the floor, but the kitty would never go near it. When it was time to go Andy picked up the cat and shoved it inside. In the process the cat scratched his right hand, and shaking his bloodied hand Andy was glad to see the saw the canvas bag move. When Andy lifted the bag, the pissed cat stare back at him through the screen, and it made Andy grin.

Andy went in the bathroom to take care of his hand, but being right handed he had a difficult time. After the wound was washed he placed Neosporin on it, but when he tried to place a Band-Aid on he always managed to dip the sticky part into the ointment and it didn't stick. When he finally finished his commitments was reaffirmed, the cat has to go.

It was too early for the clinic so he stopped at the Starbucks for his morning coffee, and being a warm day Andy couldn't leave the cat inside the car. Standing in line with the carrying case hanging from his shoulder with the damned cat inside, the kitty became the center of attention, and Andy had an urge to shove the case to someone and tell them to keep it.

He finally made it out and was at his favorite table with his coffee, his newspaper, and the damned cat. Andy placed the carrying case on the table and set his sports watch to ring in half hour so he can make his appointment. He unzipped one end of the carrying case and was waiting for the cat to jump out and run away, but the kitty contently just sat there,

"You can piss off a saint." Andy whispered, watching the cat calmly close that eye. "Why don't you just run away?" Andy said, and looking around to see if anyone saw him talking to the cat, when good looking young woman came by and looked inside the bag.

"It's a cat; oh the poor thing is blind in one eye. It looks Persian, what's her name?"

"I don't know it's not mine."

"Then who's is it?"

"I don't know."

"Did you ask inside?"

"No, you see the cat's with me."

"But you said it's not yours."

"It came to my door just before Christmas."

"Did it come with the carrying case?"

"Oh no, I bought that latter."

"You better name your cat," the woman said, and walked away.

"What an assuming bitch," Andy thought, than turned to the cat. "You can create a riot just by sitting there."

The kitty closed the one eye, if it would have said yes. Andy turned his attention to the newspaper and glanced through stories about the tragic accidents, the natural catastrophes and the school shootings. He read about the Middle East where people killing each other for the love of a Jewish God, just to prove they love it more than the Jews do. Andy went through the sport section and the short article about the Clippers. He finally got to the intellectual section and started out with Peanuts, finishing with La Cucaracha.

Andy started to solve the Sudoku, and the six by six was easy. He was about to start on the nine by nine when the kitty stick its head, and for the first time Andy saw the cat in day light. The kitty looked cute even with the bad eye, and after looking around the cat stared at Andy. The kitty slowly closed that golden eye, and Andy thought the cat was showing a sign of friendship. But he was not about to be friendly with the damned cat, Andy turned away. Someone honked a horn and when he looked up he saw Jennifer and Frank Warren waving from their car, as they drove by. Andy waved back and stood up to get a chair from the next table. When the Warrens arrived Andy and Frank knuckle punched, and Jennifer expertly removed the cat from the carrying case.

"She's a beauty," Jennifer said, cuddling the kitty. "It is a she, is it?"

"I don't know," Andy said, and Jennifer dismissed him with a wave.

"Frank, feel how soft her fur is."

Frank stroked the cat and his face light up. "It's like silk. I don't know much about cats but this could be a well-bred Persian."

"I really don't care, if you like it you can have it."

"We would, but with our schedules we won't be able to take care of it."

"It must be heart breaking,"

"Actually it is, we both grown up with animals and we miss them." Frank said.

"You lived on a farm?" Andy asked.

"No. We lived in a city with confortable surroundings and that included dogs and cats," Jennifer said, placing the kitty back into the carrying bag.

Andy didn't know what to say, just muttered.

"Did you leave on a farm?" Frank asked.

"No, I lived in L.A. all my life," Andy said.

"I can understand," Frank nodded. "I told you I traveled the world but this is where I stayed the longest."

Andy nodded. "It's a working town. "

"I almost forgot to tell you, I sold my business and we are moving to Hawaii," Frank grinned.

"Congratulation, you're the only ones I know who will successfully escape from L A," Andy asserted.

"But we do like it here," Jennifer added.

"That's what I meant. Anyway, congratulation," Andy smirked.

"Thank you," Franc said.

"What's wrong, honey?" Frank asked when he noticed, Jennifer was staring at someone.

"You see that young man with the phone?" Jennifer said.

Frank glance at the guy. "Yes, what's wrong with him?"

"He's not talking to anyone," Jennifer declared.

Andy was amazed. "Why would he do such a stupid thing?"

"He's one of the hustlers here," Jennifer said.

Andy was curious. "What kind of hustlers?"

"He's a male whore," Jennifer stated.

Andy was in disbelief. "But he's just a young man?"

"Don't feel sorry for the-dirt bags, they are merciless jerks," Franc snapped.

"Why would a woman pay money for them if they are like that?" Andy asked.

"They don't care about women, they are here for man," Frank blurted.

Andy was in shock. "Are you're kidding me?"

"No I'm not," Frank declared.

"I worked with decent, hardworking, gay people but I don't think they would be interested in this kind," Andy stated.

"You're talking about a different class of gays. This animal's hunt for lonely, old gay man who they can dominate and live off of," Jennifer declared.

Andy was dismayed. "I never heard anything like that in my entire life."

"They are everywhere," Jennifer said.

"We always had them but now the hustlers, the pimps, the whores and the pushy fags taken over the coffee shops and bother everyone. We are living the times, when you have to be careful," Frank stated.

"He's checking that old guy out, but we saw him watching you earlier," Jennifer said standing up, and left the table.

Andy watched Jennifer approaching the young man. "What is she doing?"

"Let's watch," Frank said, leaning back in his chair.

Jennifer stopped in front of the young man and when he lowered the phone to look at her, she grabbed it from his hand and lifted to her ear. "I told you the phone is dead," She said, holding the phone from the young man, who was trying to take it back.

"You bitch, give it back to me," the young man said, and Jennifer faced the young man.

"What did you say?" Jennifer asked.

"Give me back my phone," the young man said, trying to grab it.

"Do you see those gentlemen seating at my table?" Jennifer asked, and when the young man looked Frank waved.

"One more beep out of you punk and I will ask them to take care of you," Jennifer blurted. "There's no soliciting here, and if you don't want to go back to jail you better get going."

Andy watched Jennifer handing the phone back to the young man, and saw Frank ready to pounce. When the young man pocketed his phone and walked away, Andy took a deep breath. They both stood up when Jennifer returned and Frank pulled a chair out for her.

"One of these days you're going get Frank killed," Andy said to Jennifer.

"I know how to measure my victims," Jennifer stated.

Andy was skeptical. "How do you know?"

"I can recognize a predator when it's out for a meal," Jennifer affirmed.

"But don't you think it would be easier to call the police?" Andy asked.

"It's no use," Frank said. "The jail is their second home and a place where they are going to retire."

Andy was in shock. "What? I never heard of that one?"

"There are hustlers and predators on every level of our society," Frank stated.

"But why here?" Andy asked.

"I told you, male whores hang out in coffee shops, to look for gay man," Frank declared.

Andy was curious. "But how do they know who is gay?"

"They don't, so they bother everyone. They're worse than a fly," Jennifer stated.

"The decent, hardworking gays from the studios would never have anything to do with this kind," Andy assumed.

"This is like scraping the bottom of the barrel," Frank stated.

Andy shuddered. "How can a young man stoop so low?"

"I think they are the product of our educational system," Frank asserted.

Andy was skeptical. "Come on, we have great schools."

Frank nodded. "We do have great collages but our elementary education is questionable."

"The kids are stupid," Jennifer declared. "You think they would be doing this if they would have any brains?"

Andy was dumbfounded. "What about the venereal diseases, syphilis and aids?"

"Most of them are infected so they don't care," Jennifer asserted.

"Believe me, only a moron would associate with them," Frank smirked.

Andy's wrist watch buzzed and he turned it off. "I'm taking the cat to a doctor, to look at that eye," Andy said, zipping up the carrying case.

"That's wonderful," Jennifer uttered. "You see, I underestimated you."

"Now I'm not sure if it was a compliment," Andy alleged, standing up and carefully slinging the carrying case from his shoulder.

"Of course it is, you know we love you," Jennifer stated.

"I love you too," Andy waved, and left.

On his way to the clinic Andy was concerned about not checking out the place. He should have asked how much will it cost but it's too late now, and he blamed himself for not planning. Andy was hoping it won't coast more than sixty three dollars because that's all he had on him plus the emergency credit card, but hoped he will not have to use it.

When Andy arrived the building looked professional, and inside the lobby was an impressive park bench, and a table for the carrying bag. A young woman smiled from behind the desk, and when she stood up she was just the right size. She opened the carrying case, removed the kitty and cried out. "What have we here?"

Andy tried to explain. "The cat has a bad eye and would like to know what can be done?"

The woman lifted a clipboard and a pan. "No problem," she said. "You're name please?" Andy told her his name, and then she asked the cat's name, and he told her it has none. "What a pretty thing, would you like to name it?"

Andy was adamant. "Why should I, the cat is not mine."

"Just asking, is it a boy or a girl?" The woman asked.

Andy shook his head. "I don't know."

"Well, let's found out," the woman said, and expertly turned the kitty on its back. "It's hard to tell at this age," she said, and then declared. "It's a girl."

"I thought she was," Andy said, expectantly.

The woman faked a surprise. "You really thought she was a girl?"

"She behaves like a little girl," Andy proclaimed. "I'm thinking about getting her a covered litter box," Andy said, and the woman was staring at him if he was a dollar sign.

"Now let see how much she weight," she said, and placed the small cat on the scale. When the needle settled, it was just below two and a half pound. The woman placed the cat back in the carrying case then went to her desk, and turned to Andy. "If you would have a cat what would you name it?"

"Kandur, oh I'm sorry she's a girl. Priscilla, it's too long. What about Cilla."

The woman wrote it down and then handed the clipboard to Andy, and then picked up the bag with the cat and left.

There were some personal questions, and Andy only wrote down his name and address. When the woman came back he handed her the clipboard and after a glance, she hand it back. "We need your Social."

Andy shoved the clipboard back to her. "This cat is not mine, and I will only give you the necessary information, that's all."

"You right, we can live without it," the woman said. "It takes about fifteen or twenty minutes, and the veterinarian will be with you shortly. "

Andy wanted to ask what they will do to the cat for twenty minutes, when he only wanted them to check the one eye. The whole thing was out of hand, and sitting on the park bench Andy wondered if the toilet had a fire hydrant for the dogs. Finally Andy went outside to make a phone call, and was walking up and down with the phone at his ear when a car turned the corner slowly, and the driver leered at him. Andy looked at his watch, it was ten thirty in the morning and he glanced around with concern. After the phone call Andy went back inside, and very soon a guy in a white coat appeared. He introduced himself and took the other end of the bench.

The vet stared at Andy and said. "Cilla, is that her name?"

"I just named her, she's not my cat," Andy declared.

"It's a nice name, Cilla. Have I said it right?" the vet asked but didn't wait for an answer. "Do you know if Cilla had her shots?"

Andy was concerned. "What kind of shots?

The vet told Andy things he never heard before, and then told him that Cilla had flees.

"The way she scratch herself I'm not surprised," Andy quipped.

"She also has ear-mites," the vet said.

Andy was incredulous. "Ear-mites, what's that?"

The vet smiled. "It's what every stray cat has."

"What about the eye?" Andy asked.

The veterinarian smirked. "I will refer you to one of the best eye doctors in town. Now, Cilla is in a terrible shape and I wonder if you want us to take good care her, or you have another place in mind?"

"I don't know a damned thing about cats," Andy declared.

"Then don't worry Cilla is in good hands," the vet said with a reassuring grin. "As you know she's in bad shape but we'll take good care of her."

"How much will it cost?" Andy murmured.

"Let's add all this together and see what we come up with, "the vet said, and left. A few moments later the woman came back, called Andy by his first name and handed him a bill. After a glance Andy almost fainted, it was two hundred and seventy some dollars.

"Are this things are necessary?" Andy asked, and the woman nodded. "Well, if the kitty must have them then she will have them," Andy said, taking out the credit card. When she handed it back to him she also gave Andy a note with the name of the eye doctor, his address and telephone number. Another twenty minutes later a young woman in a blue uniform appeared and said. "She's a feisty one," and handed Andy the carrying case.

"Good, I don't want her to be like me," Andy declared.

"You have a nice day," the woman in blue said, and Andy could only nod.

Andy placed the carrying case on the passenger's seat, and only drove a few blocks when he heard the cat farting, followed by the awful smell. "What have they done to the cat?" Andy wondered, thinking of placing carrying case on the floor, but it was too risky in the heavy traffic. Andy was opening the windows, when a car affront of him made a sudden right turn, and Andy stepped on the break. The momentum made the carrying case tumble off the seat, and Andy knew the poor kitty just turned over in its own crap. When Andy pulled into his parking spot, he lifted the carrying case from the car and held it at arm's length. He carried it straight into the bathroom and placed it on the floor. Andy took off his watch, put on a dirty T- shirt and prepared a towel. He pulled the kitty from the carrying bag, and saw the poor thing was covered with crap. Holding the kitty by the back of the neck, he placed the small cat under the running shower, and a crying and the wiggling began. He washed the kitty clean, and in the process he was bitt five or six times, and his hand was badly scratched. Andy wrapped the cat in a towel, and as soon as he opened the door the cat jumped from him and run away to hide. With blood dripping from his wounds Andy went back to stop the bleeding and with band aids all over his hand, he was ready to leave when he almost fall over the carrying case. It was filled with the stinking stuff, and firs he got rid of the tick ones. Andy cleaned the rest with a sponge, and in the process the band aids fall from his wounds and was bleeding again. When the carrying case was cleaned, Andy hanged it from the curtain rod, and watched his blood mixed with cat shit floated down the bathtub drain.

The scratches and the bites have had a stinging sensation, and Andy placed Neosporin on his wounds. When he finally was done, Andy went in the kitchen and poured himself half a glass of rum with a touch of pear brandy, and toke a slug. He carried his drink to the couch, picked up the remote and turned on the TV. Andy looked at his wounded hands and wondered if it was worth it. So far he spent over three hundred dollars on the cat, his hands are bitten and scratched, and the cat's eye still not fixed. Andy stared at the TV, and took him a few moments to realize that he didn't understand a word, because he was watching a Spanish language broadcast.

CHAPTER 11

Andy looked at the note with the eye doctor's name, thumb tacked to his bulletin board. When he called a young lady answered, and told Andy the examination is one hundred and fifty dollars. Andy made an appointment for the following day, and right there he knew he's going to cancel it. The next day Andy got the carrying case and with the cat inside, he was on his way to the eye doctor.

When Andy arrived he gave the young lady his credit card and she charged him one hundred and fifty dollars. Andy took a seat and after a boring forty five minutes later they guided him into a white room, where the doctor with his assistant showed Andy how to handle a cat. They were truly incredible. They turned Cilla left and right, looked inside her mouth and ears and it was all done without a scratch. Andy thought the show was interesting but he didn't think it worth one hundred and fifty dollars, so he tried to enjoy it but couldn't.

Finally the doctor told Andy the cat has herpes and the eye is infected with the virus. The cataract can be removed but will return, and the operation is over four thousand dollars. Andy felt sorry for the Cilla, but he was not about to spend that kind of money on the damned cat.

It was about a week after Andy saw the four thousand dollar eye doctor, when the veterinarian who sent him there called. He wanted to have a consultation with Andy about Cilla, and they agreed to meet on the next day. When Andy arrived the veterinarian was waiting for him on the park bench, and told him he was concerned about Cilla. He asked Andy if he pronounced the cat's name right, and then he mentioned he discussed Cilla with the eye doctor, and he thinks that four thousand dollars for a reoccurring disease is too much. Since the eye can only get worse, for nine hundred dollars he can remove it.

Andy looked into the good doctors eyes and knew the son of the bitch never had the cat's welfare in mind. Being in a clinic Andy behaved like a well-trained idiot and politely told the vet that he must think about it. He was hoping his facial expression was able to camouflage the way he really felt, and driving home Andy was almost glad the kitty wound up with him.

"It takes two eyes for depth perception," Andy muttered. "If the cat can't jump than she's not a cat."

The whole thing disturbed him and to calm down Andy decided to stop at the neighborhood Starbucks to relax and think things over. Andy got his coffee and newspaper and outside his favorite table was available. Andy looked around and saw the young man with the phone, but ignored him. He couldn't help but think of how low a human being can stoop. To cheer himself Andy leafed to the intellectual section, and started out reading Peanuts. When he was done with the cartoons, Andy started to solve the Sudoku, and was right in the middle of it when a shadows fall on his newspaper. It irritated him and he looked up to see who dared, and there was Classic Face. She wore a molded, red leather pants outfit, and the

Writer was standing right next to her. With his jaws dropped Andy stood up and stared into her beautiful eyes, and then gawked at the writer's black boots, blue jeans, red tee shirt, black leather jacket and black leather Harley hat over his bleached blond hair.

"Hi, my brother told me, you two know each other," classic face said.

"From the gym," Andy stuttered.

"I'm sorry but forgot your name," the writer inquired, shaking Andy's hand.

"Andy."

"Peter," the writer said, and Andy had to control himself not to laugh. "This is my sister, Domino."

Andy shook hands with Domino. "Nice meeting you again, Andrew D Foster," Andy smiled ear to ear. He waved to them to sit down, and Domino turned to Peter. "Get me a cup of black coffee."

Peter left and Domino leaned back in her chair, crossing her shapely legs. "I see you still have the cat," Domino said, staring at Andy's scratched up hands.

Andy pulled his hands off the table. "Yeah, I couldn't get rid of it."

"And now you stuck with a one eyed cat," Domino smirked.

"How do you know?" Andy asked, than remembered the gym. "Sorry, I was such a jerk."

Domino was reassuring. "No you're not, you were honest."

"Thanks," Andy said it shyly, and Domino enjoyed that.

"So what are you going to do?" Domino inquired.

"I'm not sure," Andy shrugged. "A doctor wants to remove the cat's eye for nine hundred dollars."

"That's terrible, you should see another veterinarian?" Domino advised.

"I saw one already," Andy said. "He told me the cat is infected with the herpes virus, and even if he operates the cataract will return."

"And how much is the operation?" Domino inquired.

"It would be over three thousand dollars," Andy uttered.

"That's a lot of money for a stray cat," Domino concurred. "What are you going to do?"

"That's what I'm trying to figure out," Andy stated, when Peter came back with Domino's coffee.

"They had a mile long line," Peter complained.

"Where's yours?" Domino asked.

"Got a call from mother, she had a flat tire and left her purse at home."

"Holly shit, not again," Domino growled.

"Relax, I take care of it," Peter said, taking the keys from his pocket.

"Then hurry, you know how she is," Domino said, concerned.

"What about you?" Peter asked.

"I'll be just fine," Domino avowed.

"I'll take her home," Andy volunteered.

"Thanks man, it's Adam, right?" Peter asked.

"No, it's Andy," Andy replied.

"You right," Peter said pointing to Andy, and left.

"Don't mind my brother, he's such a pompous ass," Domino said, making Andy laugh. "And you think it's funny?"

"It's just the way you said it," Andy smirked.

"He is a selfish, self-centered pompous ass, but a brilliant writer," Domino stated.

Andy was curious. "Writers are a weird breed, is he a fag, I mean gay?"

Domino shook her head. "No, or his outfit would be red leather like mine."

"Well I'm glad," Andy affirmed.

"You have something against gays?" Domino asked.

"Ah no, I worked with some talented gay people." Andy professed. "I'm just not going around looking for their friendship."

"Peter has a girlfriend," Domino said. "He's just not mature enough to be involved emotionally."

Andy was astonished. "How his girlfriend puts up with that?"

"I don't think she noticed," Domino giggled.

"How can you have a relationship without emotional attachment?" Andy asked.

"We all went through that age, haven't you?" Domino smiled.

"I was married by that time. Have you ever been married?" Andy inquired.

Domino glanced away, shaking her head. "No. I lived with a man for almost ten years."

"At least he took care of you," Andy said, looking at her appreciatively.

"No he did not," Domino snapped. "I took care of myself."

"You did a great job, and you have an entourage to prove it," Andy smirked.

"They are just a bunch of sweet boys," Domino smirked.

"I bet," Andy said with a sour throat, and picked up his paper cup to sip his coffee.

"It was my birthday," Domino beamed. "And he sent his boys to annoy me."

"Well happy birthday," Andy said, knocking his paper cups with hers. "Who is he?"

"You mean, Anodes Tusk?" Domino asked. "He owns a gym, not the one we were in."

"Why did you break up?" Andy probed.

Domino pondered, and then she said. "He's gay."

Andy was amazed. "He's gay and you lived with him?"

"I didn't know it," Domino shrugged. "Believe me, the first five years were fun."

"Then why you stayed with him for another five years?" Andy asked.

"I quit college and run away with a man when I was eighteen years old," Domino deliberated. "It takes time to learn how to be self-sufficient."

Andy was stunned. "You run away from your family when you were eighteen?"

"You would too if you would know my family," Domino tittered.

"So what are you doing now?" Andy asked.

Domino was earnest. "I'm correcting the mistakes of the past, went back to college and made peace with my family."

Andy shook his head. "I mean for a living?"

"I was a pole dancer for a while," Domino stated.

Andy was in total shock. "Nude?"

"Completely," Domino stated when her phone ringed, and she answered. "Yes, this is Domino." She winked and covered the phone. "It's a gig, with a birthday cake."

Unwittingly Andy was listening into her business dealings, and learned that she pays two hundred dollar to each of the four guys who push the cake in with her inside, and she gets two thousand dollars for coming out, totally nude. For another thousand they can throw their cakes at her, and for another two thousand they can lick it off, with their hands tied behind their backs.

Andy was watching Domino with his jaws dropped, and when she finally was off the phone, Domino saw him staring at her like an idiot. Not knowing what to do Andy asked her about the four boys, and Domino told him they were her bodyguards, trained in the martial arts. Andy didn't know what to say and just mumbled. "You must have a fun job."

Domino shrugged. "It has its moments, but it's a job and no one can do it forever."

"Do you ever go to bed with those guys?" Andy asked with a dry throat.

"I'm coming out of a cake, not a whore house," Domino blurted, when her phone rang again. "Yes," Domino said, and her buddy stiffened. "Okay, okay, where are you? Wait, let me write it down," Domino took out a notebook and a pen from her purse and started writing but the pen didn't work. "Shit, do you have a pen?" Domino asked Andy, and she throws the used pen right in the center of a trashcan more than ten feet away.

Andy took out his pan and hand it to her. He watched her write down the address, and then tossed his pan into her purse.

"What happened?" Andy asked, watching his pen disappear.

Domino was upset. "Pete's credit card expired, and he has no cash on him."

"What are you going to do?" Andy asked.

"I must get home and get my car," Domino said, standing up.

"Where are they?" Andy asked.

Domino glanced at the note in her hand. "They are in Glendale, on Colorado near Brand."

"Come on I'll take you," Andy said standing up, and watched Domino throw her cup in the center of the trash can. When he throw his cup it hit the top edge, and the coffee flushed out covering good part of a freshly painted wall. Andy stared at his work and turned, taking the car keys from his pocket. For him walking with Domino was awkward, because she was in the center of attention. Every guy stared at her with obvious intentions, and saw Andy as the asshole with the good looking broad.

He was impressed with Domino in an awful negative way, and Andy began to believe that she was nothing more than a high class hooker. To create a distance between himself and Domino, Andy mentioned that he was married, and almost revealed his misgivings about her. When they exited the freeway, Andy turned right on Brand Avenue, and stopped on a red light. He glanced at Domino, and no matter how she made her living every part of her was chiseled beauty.

At the corner of Colorado Boulevard Andy pulled into the left turn lane, and stopped on the red light. He asked Domino to look for the car and when the light turned green Andy made the left turn onto Colorado Boulevard. Domino was watching the house numbers, and then she pointed. "There they are on the right hand side."

Andy saw a tow truck double parked, and recognized the writer's dyed blond hair under the Harley cap. He stopped behind the tow truck, and let Domino out. Andy tried to find a place to park but there was none, and made a U-turn at the next intersection. When he drove by Andy honked his horn and waved to them, and they waved back.

Their mother was standing between Domino and Peter holding a parasol, and she was dressed up like the Queen of England.

CHAPTER 12

A ndy had high hopes for the New Year but in time everything fizzled out, and he would have been back to his old routines if it was not for the cat. Sitting at his kitchen table Andy was mulling over the changes since Cilla entered his life, and the way it affected him emotionally. It seemed like that Andy had fixed amount of affections because now that he shared some with the damned cat, everything else got less. When the Clippers failed to make it into the second round of the playoffs, it didn't even bother him. Andy used to reminisce of the past but now days he only thought of Dorothy once or twice a week, and didn't think of Raymond at all. Being a God fearing man, Andy didn't know what to say to an atheist.

Andy loved Raymond like he would his own son, and talked to him like he was an adult on their long walks in Griffith Park. Raymond turned out to be a great boy with a brilliant mind, but when he chose science over basketball he disappointed everybody.

Andy heard a timid minnow, and when he looked down Cilla was there. He picked up the small cat and placed her on his lap. Stroking her Andy watched the pine needled limbs sway in the breeze, and the squirrels were chasing each other around the trunk of the crooked tree. Andy was thinking about Cilla having the herpes virus, and by licking herself she transferred the virus to her fur, and now he was stroking the kitty.

Gazing his palms with a thought the cat just infected him with the herpes virus Andy grabbed the cat by the back of the neck and throw her at least ten feet away. When Cilla landed she rushed under the couch, not knowing what was going on.

In the bathroom Andy washed his hands, examined his face in the mirror, looked into his own eyes and remembered his grandmother's warning. If you stare at yourself in the mirror long enough it will suck you in, and you will never find yourself. Andy was not superstitious but he never dared to challenge his grandmother's warnings.

Andy was thinking about being level headed and logical, so he can face the facts. First of all he has a cat in the house infected with a virus, and she's been spreading it around since Christmas. Trying to find an answer to his problem, the only thing Andy was able to come up was the song of the crucified, from the Monty Python movie Brian.

"Just look at the bright side of life," Andy mumbled the song, surrendering to his faith. He reassured himself that everything will be fine, and slowly opened the door. Andy wiped the air with his finger and tasted, scrutinizing the place. He saw the cat by the couch and got the carrying case. Andy opened it on one end and placed it on the floor. He got in his street clothes and then grabbed the cat and unceremoniously shoved her into the carrying bag. Andy zipped up the carrying case, washed his hands and drove straight to the pet clinic.

Andy told the nurse that he would like to have the cat checked for the herpes virus, and the nurse told him that first the cat has to be examined. She took the carrying case with Cilla in the back room and about ten minutes later returned. She told Andy the virus test is in two parts, one will cost ninety five dollars and the other one is ninety two and she recommends both. The nurse also told Andy that Cilla have ear mites with eggs, and the cleaning process will be an extra forty five dollars. By this time Andy was confused he agreed to everything. He handed her his credit card, to do with it whatever they decide.

When Andy got home he placed the shit box with food and water into the bathroom floor, and released the cat from the carrying case. Washed his hands and closed the door. Every time he used the toilet Andy grabbed the cat, shoved her in the carrying case and when he was done Andy released her, washing his hands every time. It was pure aggravation spiced with stupidity. If you allow a living thing into your house, you also let in the guests they carry.

Andy was tossing and turning all night, practically in pain from paranoia. The next day the phone rang, it was the clinic. The woman told Andy the cat was free from the herpes virus, and only the left eye was infected. But the cat is run down and needs supplements, and that will be another forty four dollars an fifty two cents. But Andy didn't care, he was happy to release the cat from the toilet with a sigh.

"Better be safe than sorry," Andy mumbled, and place everything back where they were. Sitting by the kitchen table Andy watched Cilla come in the kitchen, and he picked her up. The kitty cuddled up to him, not knowing what will be next.

On the following day right after his morning walk in Griffith Park, Andy stopped by the pet clinic to pick up Cilla's supplements, and decided to stop in a pet shop. Through the connecting door

Andy walked into the pet store and was impressed by a large water tank, filled with exotic fishes.

In the cats section Andy saw a wood box sticking out on the end of an isle and it was filled with sand. A young lady worked nearby and Andy asked her about the sand, and she told him it was cat litter. Thinking of the colorful pebbles he bought for the cat, Andy became light headed and was wondering if that's how stupidity felt like. Learning from his own mistakes was really hard on him, and Andy was holding onto the wood box, trying to get himself out of his mental state he trapped himself in.

Staring at the sand Andy asked the young lady if the litter in the box was any good, and she reassured him it was excellent. When Andy saw the shelves filled with cat litter, there was too many to choose from and the young lady explained. They have scented and unscented litter and they are all clumpy. Andy didn't understand the clumpy part, so she explained that clumpy sand has less dust.

"How come I didn't think of that?" Andy exclaimed, choosing a 42 pound scented, low dust clumpy formula, and carried it at least twenty feet to his shopping cart.

He was pushing the cart around and bought a plastic litter strainer, a two sided brush and some plastic and stainless steel dishes. On his way to the cash register Andy saw the young lady who helped him earlier, and asked her if they have anything to pour the cat litter into, and she led him right to it. Andy selected one with a cover for privacy, and with a full shopping cart Andy headed to the checkout stand. He paid with a credit card and didn't even bother to check how much it cost.

At home, Andy took the cardboard box with the colorful pebbles the cats used in Xanadu and the Taj Mahal, and threw it out. He sat the litter box in its place and poured in some of the cat litter. When Andy was done Cilla showed up, and climbed inside to use it.

After a long shower Andy got into his lounge outfit, made a mug of hot green tea with lemon, honey, and thickened it with a healthy shut of spiced rum. Sipping his brew Andy headed to the couch, and just got comfy when the source of all his troubles showed up. She glared at him with that golden eye, than started grooming herself.

"The first thing we're going to do is fix that eye," Andy said stroking Cilla. The kitty pushed her head against the palm of his hand, but Andy was not in the mood to be friendly with the damned cat. He picked up his mug, sipped his tea, and was hoping for a future without cats.

CHAPTER 13

Andy was feeding the cat with the supplements, and in the process he got scratched and was bit several times. A few days later he was sitting outside at the Starbucks Coffee, when Frank the oldest person in the building walked by and stopped for a chat.

"Did you hear about Frank and Jennifer, they are moving to Hawaii?" Old Frank said.

"They told me," Andy replied.

The old man leaned on his cane. "Why don't you move out there?"

"I was born and raised right here in LA, but at your age you should go," Andy said.

Old Frank shook his head. "I can't, the doctors who keep me alive are all here."

"You have no umbilical cord to them," Andy quipped.

"Yes I do. I'm their prisoner forever," old Frank said, lighting a cigarette.

"When are you going to give that up?" Andy asked.

"Never, it would kill me," old Frank said laughing and coughing, and then swallowing what he just coughed up.

Andy liked the old guy he just couldn't stand his disgusting habits. Old Frank was a fascinating character, he lost part of his lungs but smokes two packs of cigarettes a day, drinks frozen tequila and breaths oxygen.

"I haven't seen you lately, what are you doing with yourself?" Andy asked.

"I don't know if I ever told you that I was a horse man, and I go to the track quite often. Got a tip the other day and wanted to place two hundred on its nose but chickened out, and only had it for twenty," old Frank said coughing, and Andy turned away.

Old Frank stared at Andy's scratched up hands. "What happened to your hands?"

Andy looked at his hands, covered with bandages and black and blue marks. "I have this cat and tried to feed her the medication."

Old Frank checked his watch. "Got to go, doctor's appointment," than pointed with his cane. "There's a pet store in the corner, I think it's called Pet Mania. They are nice people go in and talk to them." Old Frank strode away and then stopped. "Have you ever tried mix the medication with the cat food?"

Andy stared at old Frank like a zombie, and then his bruised hands and mumbled. "Mixing the medicine with the cat food?"

Andy tried to finish the Sudoku but his mind just wasn't there. He made a mistake and was ready to tear the newspaper into little pieces. Andy glanced in the direction of the pet store, folded the newspaper and shoved it under his arm. With coffee cup in hand Andy decided to visit the place, but first he walked by to check it out. On the corner he threw his coffee cup into the trashcan, turned around and went for it.

Andy pulled open the glass door and walked in. Looking around he stroked the statue of a small brown dog on top of a glass display case, and felt the warmth if it was alive. Andy looked around but everyone was busy, and he stroked the dog again when he realized it was alive, but was frozen stiff. When a young man came Andy asked him what's wrong with the dog, and the young man told him that it was abused.

Gently stroking the doggy, Andy couldn't understand what a beautiful small dog can possibly do to be driven into this state. Shaking his head Andy gently stroked it one more time, and thought he saw the eyes move. "Poor thing, I've never seen anything like this before."

"I've seen worse," the young man stated. "There are real mental cases out there. What can I help you with?"

Andy stroked the small dog one more time, and he thought he saw the eyes moved. "A cat came to my door and I took it in. Her left eye is infected with the herpes virus, and I wonder if you could tell me what I should do."

The young man scratched his head. "I don't know much about them, but here comes Janette."

"Can I help you?" Janette smiled.

"Just before Christmas a small cat came to my door, and her left eye is infected with the herpes virus. Do you know a doctor who could help?"

"Herpes is very common with cats," Janette stated. "I treat it with Lysine."

Andy was surprised. "You mean Lysine, the amino acid?"

"Yes," Janette replied.

Some costumers came in and Janette told Andy to feel free to look around, and she went to help out the new arrivers. Walking around, Andy saw cats, dogs, birds and rabbits, and they were all live individuals with a need. Andy became so found of them it was almost intimidating. He stopped at the cage with three adorable kittens, each one about three inches long, including their tails. Andy watched them take up their defensive positions with threatening cries. If he would have lived in the old house he would have taken them right away, but now he could only hope a good family will fall in love with them, just like he did. Leaving the store Andy wished them well, and hoped they would wound up with some nice people.

Andy went to Dana's drugstore, to get a bottle of Lysine, and a bag of cotton squares. When Andy got home Cilla was waiting for him by the door, and he picked her up. He had an urge to squeeze the cuddly thing but was afraid to hurt her, so he placed the kitty on the top of his now scratched up leather couch, and gently stroked the Cilla's soft fur. He was thinking of the ones he saw in the cages, and was glad for this one being free.

On his next trip to the super market Andy picked up the eighty dollar, five foot tall scratching post, with three landings.

CHAPTER 14

After a busy day Andy decided stay home for the evening and changed into his lounge pence, tee shirt and wool slippers. Made his usual green tea and after he tasted his brew, Andy clicked his tong, wiped the inside of his mouth and shuddered with joy.

In the living room Andy placed his tea-mug on the coffee table, took his place in the center of the couch and turned on the TV. It was May the First, and people was marching in every major city around the world.

On the Universal Studios' lot Andy worked with the true magicians of the craft, and he respected their knowledge. But being in management and on the other side the coin, Andy tried to take the most out of them for the least amount of money. He knew the game was fixed because he personally rigged many contracts himself, and his final handshake was always with his heartfelt sympathy. Andy remembered the names and faces of the many people he knew, and with a smirk he turned the TV off. He didn't like to see people march in their street cloths, without the floats or the marching bands.

It was normal for Andy, to mix the day's reality with his illusions, and leaning back into the soft leather of his sofa, Andy recalled his first May day with Dorothy.

They were young with full of hopes for a better world, and they were against the Vietnam War. Back then they had long hair, wore necklaces with a peace sign, and their sympathy with the people of Vietnam was borderline treason. It was a cool sunny May Day when Andy took Dorothy to the Huntington Library, and was pleased when the place impressed her. They gawked at the drawings from around the world, depicting the way our imagination worked throughout the ages, and the way the giants of science replaced those illusions with authenticity. They saw Isaac Newton's Mathematica Principia, and admired the libraries' many original Bibles, written by hand. There was also a Guttenberg Bible, The Birds of America, an Audubon's masterpiece and Chaucer's Canterbury Tales. The library also has Shakespeare's First Folio edition of his collected plays, from 1623, and altogether the library has about 150 rear books, letters and works of importance.

Andy enjoyed showing Dorothy all the precious arts and works of knowledge, in a beautiful setting. When they got to the cactus garden Dorothy felt like she was in another world, and they even enjoyed the steep climb among the cactuses, from around the world.

When they got to the top near the entrance Andy inhaled, and when he looked around his living room he was able to see Dorothy catching her breath with a cheerful smile, before she faded away.

Sipping his tea Andy slowly got back into reality, and noticed Cilla with her tail up, rubbing herself to his leg. She was whining like something was wrong with her, and he picked Cilla up to check her out. Thinking she eats something poisonous Andy rushed in the kitchen and checked her food but it was untouched. Andy found the empty can in the garbage and smelled it; there was nothing wrong with it. Not knowing what to do Andy was hoping the cat's trouble will just go away, but a few days later other cats begin to gather and Andy thought they heard her cry. Cilla's behavior became so unbearable Andy grabbed her and pushed the cat into the carrying bag. He drove to Pat Mania, and Andy placed the carrying case on the glass counter. He unzipped one end, and Cilla poked her head out. When Janette approached with a group of people, Cilla retreated.

Andy and Janette greeted each other and she removed Cilla from the carrying case. "So this is the kitty?" Janette said, and Andy was surprise to see how tame Cilla was.

"Yeah, that's the one," Andy said looking at his hands, decorated with her latest bites.

"She came to his door last year," Janette said to the group and then she turned to Andy. "Just before Christmas, am I right?" Janette asked and Andy nodded. "And he toke it in for the night," Janette chuckled, and everyone laughed.

"Just feel how soft her fur is," Janette added, and they begin to stroke the cat.

Andy watched Cilla enjoying herself, but when a young boy pulled her tale he picked up the carrying case. "Janette, may I talk to you?" Andy asked, than looking at the group he added. "I can wait."

"Sure," Janette said, placing Cilla back in the bag, and zipped up the opening. She went behind the counter to take care of the people, and Andy with the carrying case hanging from his shoulder, roamed around. He picked up some more treats for the cat, and by the time he returned, Janette was free and Andy paid for the treats. He completely forgot what he came fore when Janette asked him. "You wanted to ask me something?"

"Oh yes," Andy said. "Something's wrong with the cat."

"What do you think it is?" Janette inquired.

Andy shrugged. "I have absolutely no idea,"

"Then how do you know something's wrong?" Janette asked.

Andy was flustered. "She whines and cries, rubbing herself to my leg. I mean a real nuisance."

"How old you think she is?" Janette asked.

Andy shrugged. "She came to my door before Christmas, and was less than three pounds."

Janette said. "Now it's May, I think it's about time"

Andy didn't understand. "It's time for what?"

Janette smiled. "She's in heat."

Andy didn't know what she meant. "What do you mean?"

Janette repeated. "She's in heat!"

Andy finally got it. "Ah, you mean in heat?"

"Yes," Janette smiled.

Andy was skeptical. "But she was just a small thing. I could hold her in one hand."

Janette nodded. "They do grow fast."

Andy felt frustrated. "What can I do?"

"Nothing," Janette said. "When it's over and she's back to normal, Cilla has to be spayed."

"I'm sorry, I don't know what you're talking about," Andy stated.

"They fix her so she can't have babies." Janette explained.

Andy was concerned. "What are they going to do to her?"

"They remove her ovaries," Janette said with a grave smile.

Andy was stunned. "That's too drastic; I think she would make a good mother."

Janette was surprised. "You want more cats?"

95

"No, I don't even want this one," Andy blurted.

Janette was surprised. "You want to get rid of her?"

Andy was resolute. "Yes. I have no place for her."

Janette shrugged. "Than what are you worry about?"

"I want to make sure everything's done right," Andy confessed.

Janette was dubious. "And after all that you still want to get rid of her?

"Yes. What's wrong with that?" Andy exclaimed.

"I just asked?" Janette smiled.

Andy thought she was mocking him and said. "Thanks for the advice."

Andy didn't care for her assumptions when he hardly knew her, and she definitely didn't know him. His irritation just got worst when he forgot where he parked his car, and blamed himself for not making a mental note. Andy toke the car keys from his pocket and pushed the button. To his surprise the car behind him blew its horn. First he didn't want to believe it but after a closer scrutiny Andy recognized his car. So he pushed the button one more time just to make sure.

Andy placed the carrying case on the passenger's floor. More than four month gone by, and after all the money and time he spent, not counting the scratches and bites, the cat is still blind in one eye and now she was in heat.

CHAPTER 15

One day when Cilla laid on her back and when Andy rubbed her belly, she bit his hand' Andy rushed to the bathroom to clean the wound knowing it was a love bite, but it pissed him up. The damned cat just can't go around showing her affection with bites.

Andy had absolutely no idea what to do or how to go about it, accept he was pissed and he decided to go with being pissed. He showed his hand to the cat and told her she bites and the cat hissed, and that made Andy really mad. He hollered at the cat, telling her she bites again and again, scaring the small thing, and made her run under the couch to hide. Andy was so furious he picked up one end of the couch and banged it to the floor, and then he picked up his wooden back scratcher and hit the couch's legs till he heard Cilla's cry.

He recalled the small brown dog in the pet shop suffering from mental cruelty, and feeling guilty Andy throw the backscratcher on the coffee table. He heard of animal rights and tried to respect the damned cat, but it was not easy to communicate with her and Cilla was taking its precious time to learn.

Looking out the window Andy knew Cilla was not the problem, he was still under Domino's spell, and sometimes he visualized her in that skintight red leather outfit. It was obvious she was a great looking woman but when he compared her to an art work, he could only come up with a nude statue of a beautiful girl, complemented with pigeon drops.

To avoid running into Domino, Andy stopped going to the gym and moved his exercise to Griffith Park. Andy believed that his moral standards kept him being a decent human being, and he was not about to give it up or lift her up to his.

The thirty two years he spent with Dorothy bounded them together, and he was ready to spend for the rest of his life with her memory. To wipe Domino from his mind Andy visited the places he enjoyed with Dorothy, and being in the middle of April, he went to Descanso Gardens, just to push his nose into the lilac blossoms.

When Dorothy saw kids smell the flowers it was an emotional experience. Sometimes her eyes dwelled with tears, and Andy had to walk her to the Japanese Tea House were they could sit down and he could comfort her. They never discussed their desire to have children, and it was the only blemish in their otherwise perfect marriage. The two of them were very different in many ways, but spiritually they were one.

Andy also loved to visit the Los Angeles Botanic Garden on Baldwin Avenue, next to the Santa Anita race track, but Dorothy couldn't stand the sound of peacocks and they only visited the place on special occasions.

Now it was the end of April, and Andy was happy to make his annual pilgrimage to The Huntington. Andy was driving on the 210 Freeway going east. In Pasadena he drove past Lake Avenue and then he pulled into the right lane to get off on Hill Street. Andy stayed on the road next to the freeway till he got to Allen Street, and then turned right. He drove straight down to San Marino his old neighborhood, and on the end of Allen Street Andy stopped at the stop sign. When he crossed the road, Andy entered through the ornate gates into The Huntington Library, Art Collections and Botanic Gardens.

Andy found a shaded spot on the parking lot's Bamboo Road, and locking the doors he glanced in the direction of the place where he grown up. Of course he couldn't see the house from where he was but he knew it was there. Turning around he looked up at Mount Wilson Observatory, where from Edwin Hubble used to view the universe.

Andy got his sticker at the member's window, and almost rushed to the rose garden. After he smelled some of the flowers, Andy toke some pictures of the rose covered road and in an alcove he rested on a bench. With his eyes closed Andy inhaled the aroma emitted by the blossoms, and when he opened his eyes their overflowing colors filled his sight and mind. Before he continued Andy winked and smiled at the stone bench, and then took a photo of it. On the end of the rose canopied road two small stone lions guarded the entrance to the Japanese garden, and Andy took a picture of them and then. He walked down the wooden steps to a covered dirt road, holding on to the natural wood handrails. Andy photographed the Moon Bridge crossing a lake, and the tea house up on the hillside. He stopped to admire the huge bell, with its large wooden striker and then walked the dirt road to the back of the Chinese garden. Andy entered the pagoda roofed building through a circular door, and at the Chinese restaurant he bought some chicken and rice. Andy found a table by the lake and enjoying the beautiful surroundings, he finished the plate.

Andy would have loved to go through the library or to see the cactus garden but it was getting cloudy, and the weatherman forecasted showers. He headed to the mansion and on the first floor Andy stopped in an alcove to pay his respect to two men, who helped to nudge us into modern times. On the left was the small portrait of the myopic Samuel Johnson by Joshua Reynolds. Johnson's dictionary helped the English language turn into the language of science. Facing it on the other wall was James Watt, by Henry Raeburn. Watt's steam engine triggered the industrial revolution that created a new working class, required to know how to read and write.

The main gallery walls are decorated with the life sized paintings of the rich and famous of their days, by the leading artists of their time. The collection does have a few paintings by Thomas Gainsborough, and his masterpiece The Blue Boy is in the center of the far wall. It depicts a young man in his blue knickerbockers, holding his fathered hat in his right hand and his left knuckles on his waist. He casually placed his left foot forward to declare. "I'm here."

On the other wall facing The Blue Boy is Pinkie, by Thomas Lawrence, portraying a young girl in a pink outfit as she just finished a pirouette. It was their favorite, and Dorothy believed that watching an old painting of a young girl, is like being in another dimension within an alternate reality.

Andy went to the ornate terrace, it was raining and he inhaled the fresh air. He pushed two chairs together at the edge, and seat on the one on the left. Watching the lush landscape through a curtain of rain, Andy knew if he would rich over to the chair next to his, he would be able to touch her because Dorothy was with him all day, every step of the way.

CHAPTER 16

A few days later the cat's behavior became so unbearable Andy's patients came to the low end. To calm himself Andy made green tea and enriched it with a generous amount of spiced rum, but it wasn't enough. He finally went to the bookcase and removed one of Sam's present. Andy got a porcelain saucer to use it for an ashtray, and lit the joint. Andy was enjoying himself when Cilla came in the kitchen with her tail up, and moaned like a bitch in heat. She rubbed herself into Andy's leg.

"Get away from me," Andy said, pushing Cilla away. But she refused, and the cat's aggression startled Andy. He stomped his foot on the floor like his grandmother used to do, and said "sheetz." The cat hissed but run away, and Andy turned his chair back to the table and lit the joint. He looked out the window when a bird landed on the crooked tree. The wind blew the branch but the bird was holding on with its talons, steadying itself with its wings. Andy watched the bird move its head in rapid motion, jumped on another branch and then flew away. He envied the bird for its three dimensional freedom, then remembered how fragile they must be so they can fly.

"I'm already fragile, and I don't mind being on good old terra firma," Andy murmured, placing his tea mug on the table. He lit the joint again and tried to hold his breath like Sam, but it made him cough. Enjoying his state of mind Andy came to the conclusion that Sam was right, and was thankful for his presents. Somehow Sam always knew how to treat people, and many of the leaders in the spectator sports industry respected his advice. Being neighbors and friends all through the years Andy learned that Sam was a fierce competitor, but a gentle giant. Sam was full of love, and he spread around his family and friends. When he talked about his competitors it was always with respect, and his teammates knew they can depend on him.

Andy took a hit but the joint was out, and lighting it he slightly burned his hand. In the sink he placed his hand under the running water and feeling the cold liquid running through his fingers, Andy realized that he was stoned. Drying his hands with a paper towel, Cilla was rubbing herself to his leg.

"Sorry, I can't help you," Andy said, and squashed the paper towel into a ball. He aimed at the trashcan but missed it by more than a foot. It made him wonders if his bad aim was the reason they called him the klutz, in the Universal's Black Tower.

Andy watched Cilla jump on the paper ball. "At least somebody's having fun," Andy thought, lighting the joint and taking two more puffs out of it. He held the joint under the running water, and dropped the wet but into the garbage can,

He's tension went back to Cilla, and couldn't help but sympathize with the cat. "You poor thing, first they wanted one of your eyes and now they want you're ovaries. What have you done to deserve all that?"

Andy was so stoned he wished the kitty would understand what he was saying. "I forgot you don't have to do a damned thing."

Andy was looking for his mug, and found where he left it. Tasting the lukewarm liquid he watched Cilla play with the paper ball, and noticed how much she grown. And even with her left eye shut, Cilla was a good looking cat.

"Do you know you're a beautiful young lady," Andy said to Cilla. "With your eye fixed you will be gorgeous, and then I will give you a way to someone I can trust."

With an urge to cuddle the kitty Andy put down his mug and picked her up by the back of her neck. Cilla omitted an indignant cry, and Andy realized that this is not the way to pick up a young lady. "Okay, okay," Andy apologized. "The next time I'll use both hands."

Andy thought the cat was too cuddly so he placed her on the table and to his surprise Cilla didn't whine. She calmly walked to the window and sit on the ledge.

"Holy shit, you're back to normal," Andy shouted.

He was glad that Cilla was not horny anymore, but now she was ready to be spayed and Andy wasn't sure if it was the right thing to do. If the cat can't have babies then it's about life and death, and Andy wanted to believe in an unwritten law but didn't know any. And finally conclude that ignorance was no bliss.

Andy was stoned and it was getting too complicated, so he took a break from his mental activity. He made some more green tea, with lemon, honey, and only poured in the spiced rum for taste. The process made him forget his troubles and watched the Cilla calmly walk to the window ledge. Outside the light breeze moved the pine needled branches on the crooked tree, and Andy noticed that everything was back to normal. Being stoned Andy enjoyed everything he thought, did or saw and it was all entertainment.

CHAPTER 17

The next morning when Andy opened his eyes and Cilla was staring at him from less than a foot away. He wanted to hit the damned cat but it was too fast, jumped off the bed and disappeared. Going through his morning chores no matter what he did the cat was in his mind, and begin to think of cats as a useless responsibility, that eats, shits and bites.

Later in the day Andy went grocery shopping and after he parked his car, he decided to stop at Pat Mania. This time he made a mental note where he parked his car, and went in the store where Janette just finished with a costumer. Andy came right to the point. "Why the cat has to be spayed?"

"You told me you don't want cats."

"No, I don't," Andy cried.

"Then you should take her to be spayed," Janette stated.

"Is it legal?" Andy asked.

Janette chuckled. "Of course it is. Do you have any idea what would happen if we won't spay them?"

Andy scratched his head. "I'm just not sure if it's the right thing to do."

Jeanette clarified. "Of course it is. Her whining will drive you crazy."

"It already has," Andy wailed.

"And it will happen three or four times a year. Believe me she can make you miserable, because she is miserable," Janette explained.

Her phone went off and Janette excused herself. Andy went to browse around and when he returned a small crowd gathered around the cash register. They were talking about an accident just happened on the corner of Laurel Canyon and Ventura Boulevards.

"We just drove by and it's a mass," a man said.

"The friend of mine told me it was Frank," Janette confirmed. "He used to come in here,"

"You mean Frank, Frank Warren?" Andy asked.

"His name was Warren?" Janette asked.

"Yes," Andy said. "I just had coffee with them. Does his wife know?"

Janette was amused. "I didn't know he was married?"

"Oh yes. She's just a wonderful woman," Andy implied.

Janette was amazed. "You're kidding?"

Andy noticed a short, baldheaded lawyer type twitting to someone.

"How did he die?" Andy asked.

Janette stared at Andy with a slight smile. "He stepped affront of a buss full of people, reading the Dailey Racing Form."

Andy's his face lights up. "You said he was reading the Dailey Racing Form?"

Janette stared at him. "Yes. Why?"

"It was not Frank Warren," Andy shouted. "The bus didn't run over Frank Warren, it was old Frank, I can't remember his last name."

"You just said his name was Frank Warren," Janette inquired.

"I made a mistake," Andy corrected himself. "I thought you were talking about Frank. You see Frank Warren is a nice middle aged guy with a beautiful wife, and Old Frank is just a disgusting old man."

Andy didn't realize what he just said till he looked around and saw all the dumbfounded faces staring at him.

"Ah, forget it," Andy shouted and rushed out of the store.

He went by two women talking about old Frank Warren and his huge family, but Andy was in such a hurry that he was on the far end of the parking lot when he remembered where he parked his car.

CHAPTER 18

Driving east on Riverside Drive, Andy remembered not buying the groceries and now he was afraid to go home because he might take it out on the cat. Andy drove by Patty's restaurant but Dorothy and Patty were good friends, and he was not in the mood to remember how many cigarettes Patty smoked before she died of cancer.

Andy parked behind the Falcon Theatre owned by Garry Marshall, and with newspaper in armpit he walked to Priscilla's coffee house. Inside there's always a line, but Andy didn't mind the wait because the place is so unique. After he got his coffee Andy went outside and found a table with a green umbrella for shade. When he opened the newspaper Andy went directly to the intellectual section, and start reading the Peanuts cartoons. He was in a mood to sympathize with Charley Brown. Andy also found the Art Buckwald article funny, and very interesting. When he looked up Andy saw five gorgeous women crossing the street, four of them in skirts and blouses but the fifth had a gray pants suit on that fit her like a glove. Andy recognized Domino and lifted the newspaper to cover his face, but he distinctly heard one of the young women mentioned his name. Andy was still hiding behind the newspaper when Domino stopped affront of him and pulled the paper away.

"Well, hello stranger," Domino said. "I never had a chance to thank you for the ride."

"I was glad to do it," Andy said, standing up.

"So, what are you up to?" Domino asked.

"Just reading the newspaper," Andy said, pulling the paper from her hand. "Believe me there's nothing in it that would interest you."

"Can I get you anything?" Domino asked.

Andy shook his head. "I'm fine."

Domino left and Andy wondered if she's going to come back. When he looked after her Andy saw the guys at the other tables fallowed her with burning eyes, and openly displayed intentions. He got back to his newspaper and was reading the sport section when Domino returned. Andy placed the paper aside and stood up to help her with the chair.

Domino placed her paper cup and a paper tray with coffee cake on the table. She pulled the chair close and with a plastic fork she cut off a piece of cake and placed it close to Andy's mouth. "Would you like to have some of this?" Domino asked, pushing the fork with the cake so close to his mouth, Andy had no other choice but to eat the damned cake.

"No more," Andy said firmly, holding one hand up and wiping his mouth with the other. And Domino watched him with her lingering stare.

Regaining his composure Andy asked. "What happened to the ladies I saw you with?"

"They are on their way to work," Domino stated.

"I heard one of them recognized me. Believe me I'm not that famous."

"Yes you are," Domino stated. You and Dorskin were the two brilliant ghosts of Universal Studios, and only answered to Lou Wasserman."

Andy was surprised. "Dorskin was my mentor, and he was not a ghost."

"Dorskin wrote some of the most important laws for the Motion Picture industry, and not many people knew about it." Domino stated.

"Yes I know," Andy said.

"But you were the brain behind everything else," Domino stated.

Andy shook his head. "Not true, I can't even remember where I parked my car."

"Don't be so modest," Domino quipped. "Some people think you created the Hollywood Labyrinth, and others whispered that you were the Labyrinth."

Andy wanted to change the subject. "I think your mind is infested with tabloid garbage."

"I didn't learn it from the tabloids," Domino stated. "By the way, why they call you The Great Scott?"

"My great grandparents came from Scotland and The Great Scott was a restaurant on Los Feliz Boulevard," Andy explained.

"My father used to take us there for diner," Domino said. "He told me that you used to wipe your feet in the small replica of a British by the entrance."

Andy shook his head. "Wrong. I do like the British and I broke with that custom a long time ago. By the way, who is you're father."

"Monty Sylliphant," Domino replied. "You worked with him at Universal."

Andy was stunned. "Monty is your father? Oh mine, his office was right next to mine on the twelfth floor. How's he doing?"

Domino sighed. "He passed away about four years ago."

"Sorry to hear that, he was the best looking man in the black tower, and the women loved him," Andy revealed.

"Yes I know, but he still was my father," Domino acknowledged.

What a small world Andy thought, remembering Domino with her brother and their mother standing on the sidewalk on Colorado Boulevard. And came to realize why Monty never had his family's pictures out on his desk.

"He was my hero," Andy reminisced. "I can never forget his retirement speech, he left us in stiches."

Domino nodded. "I heard about it."

Andy was amazed. "Do you know how he used to close the meetings?"

Domino shook her head. "No, I've never been in any of them."

Andy pulled up his shoulders, pointed with his finger and changed his voice. "Be careful out there, stupidity is contagious."

"Oh yes," Domino remembered. "We watched the cup show, where the captain sends out his troops with a warning."

Andy was curious. "How come he never mentioned you?"

Domino became subdued, and shrugged. "I was an outcast."

"Well, I can't blame him," Andy stated.

"I do deserve some kind of understanding, after all he was my father," Domino uttered.

"It's not easy to understand a morally loose juvenile delinquent," Andy said in a reprimanding tone.

Domino chuckled with her sideway stare. "I don't think I deserve that."

"My opinion is based on what I heard from you," Andy stated with a firm stare.

Domino was stunned. "I must have painted a dreary picture of myself."

"Yes, a morally loose one," Andy said with a somber tone.

Domino became agitated. "You think I'm immoral?"

"What do you want me to say to a person who solicits sex?" Andy bellowed.

Domino was astounded. "Do you know what you just called me?"

"Don't play the innocent with me," Andy roared. "I was sitting right next to you when you discussed every act, and how much will it cost."

Domino was furious. "You think coming out of a cake is sex?"

"Yes, if you're nude and letting some strangers lick your body," Andy declared.

"Your moral code needs some updating. We have long passed the days when a woman's ankle was a sexy sight," Domino said with fury.

"There's nothing wrong with my moral code," Andy confirmed.

"Then you must be one of those who want to see woman covered from top to toe," Domino shouted.

"We had girls coming out of birthday cakes, but they wore a bikini." Andy stated.

"Yeah, there's a song about those itsy bitsy ones," Domino smirked.

"Are you against them," Andy glared. "Or you rather see everyone runaround naked like you do?"

"Only a hypocrite would think that a sensuous play done by a woman in a controlled environment is wrong," Domino sneered. "But it was alright when you deed it."

Andy was stunned. "What do you mean by that?"

"I heard about you guys running around naked on the USC campus," Domino scoffed.

"Don't throw at me a stupid initiation ritual. It was a long time ago and we didn't do it for the money," Andy stated.

"For the money you've bought up intellectual properties as cheaply as possible, and paid off people to protect the Studio's interest," Domino declared.

Andy shrugged. "It was my job."

"Let's get back to your streaking. How do you think your fellow female students felt about it?"

"I bet they loved it," Andy wisecracked.

"How do you know?"

"So I don't. I told you it was a stupid initiation."

"Half the world's population is women, and you don't care what we think?" Domino exclaimed.

Andy was annoyed, but couldn't let her dictate. "Why do you have to exaggerate?"

"Your moral values are to restrict women's rights," Domino stated with an unyielding stare. "And that's not an exaggeration,"

Andy was outraged. "How could you say such a thing, our moral values guides our civilization?"

"Your moral values are made up by man to benefit themselves," Domino spit back.

Andy shrugged. "We are not perfect, but we do our best."

Domino was astounded. "You had time since the beginning of civilization, and just look what you've done."

"Glad to," Andy said with a gracious gesture. "We have toilet facilities and electricity in every home. We have fast transportation, air travel and you can communicate with everyone, everywhere in the world from where you are seating. Now what's wrong with that?"

"Those are technological achievements and would have occurred no matter what," Domino replied

"You think you women could have done it better?" Andy smirked.

"During the Second World War woman did all the work under terrible circumstances, and we all survived. With your leadership there's nothing's sacred, wars follow wars and your frustration with women is clearly demonstrated in the way you turned sex into a commodity," Domino exclaimed.

"And what you are doing will save us from all that," Andy smirked.

"This is your world and if there's a market, I have the merchandise." Domino smiled, lifting her torso, and slightly moved it left to right.

Andy couldn't tear his eyes off of her breasts, but the subject was too serious and it was not easy to explain it to a morally corrupt woman. When Andy was able remove his eyes from her beautiful mounds, he mumbled. "You are so misguided."

"Everyone in the world is misguided, and quite a few profit from it," Domino confirmed.

"I will not going to apologize for doing well," Andy avowed.

"Wealth is just part of your system's inequality," Domino blurted. "Made up with phony birthrights by a bunch of inbreed idiots who created a polluted world, filled with hunger and suffering."

Domino's fierce outburst was a surprise to Andy. "I've told you, we are not perfect."

"Is that your excuse for purposely misguiding people?" Domino asked.

Andy looked away. There are a lot of people who fall into the traps he set in his ruthless business dealings.

"But that's not all," Domino continued. "Under your male leadership everyone is manipulated with stupid ideas, and to defend it you are ready to march into a nuclear war."

"It's in our nature to defend ourselves," Andy stated.

"The survival of our species depends on our intellect, and not on our primitive urges or desires?" Domino declared.

"You're right," Andy admitted. "We are constantly learning and we have a long way to go, but we always correct our mistakes."

"Like collecting all the nuclear waste and dumping them into the oceans?" Domino exclaimed. "When all goes to hell and those barrels fall apart, just wait for the next hurricane to pick up that water mixed with radioactive waste, and rain it on the land."

"I'll never hear about that," Andy said with a terrified tone.

"It's the worst thing we've have done besides dropping them," Domino stated.

"So you think woman could have done it better? Andy probed.

"In nature males provides protection and make sure there's enough young running around, but the matriarchs lead the packs." Domino explained.

Andy nodded. "Okay, than let's move more women into politics."

"It's not that easy," Domino shrugged. "In every society they raise their girls to please man. Brainwashed and abused people must be liberated, and then they have to learn how to control their own lives before they can govern others."

Andy knew some actresses who didn't know themselves, and imitated the favored character they played. "Well, we are not perfect but we do have some fine institutions of learning, and I don't see any shortage of women there.

"Schools are as good as what they teach," Domino declared

"I know where you are coming from. You're one of those Darwinists who don't believe that we are created in the image of God?" Andy exclaimed.

"I do believe in evolution," Domino declared. "And let me surprise you, we are still evolving and it has nothing to do with God."

"Have it ever occurred to you that evolution can be one of God's mysterious ways?" Andy smirked.

"Why do we have a mysterious God," Domino inquired. "When he only help us when we help ourselves?"

"Because God is everywhere," Andy gestured with a reassuring smiled. "It's within you and it's within me. I can't even imagine this universe without God."

"Do you know what's funny?" Domino quipped.

"Enlighten me," Andy smirked.

"Atheist feels the same way about the universe as you do about your God," Domino smirked. "But when they look up, they see a lot more than you do."

Andy's eyes narrowed, "you sound like an atheist."

"Why, do you know one?" Domino quarried.

Andy shrugged and looked away. "Yes, my Godson is an atheist."

"Your Godson is an atheist?" Domino snickered.

Andy didn't get the joke and was getting irritated. "So what else are you doing with yourself besides coming out of cakes, totally naked?"

Domino shook her head. "I stopped doing that."

"I thought you loved it?" Andy hissed.

"I had enough fun," Domino said. "I let others enjoy it and I just count the money."

"The four ladies I saw you with, are working for you?" Andy asked.

"Not really," Domino stated. "They work for themselves and I arrange the clientele for a fee. By the way they are for hire, now don't tell me you can't afford them?"

Andy was annoyed. "No thanks. You should worry about yourself with all the free time you have."

"I'm back in college and working on my masters in psychology," Domino stated.

Andy was not convinced. "How do you manage that with all those boyfriends around?"

"I stopped being approachable for quiet sometime," Domino said.

Andy didn't understand. "Are you in-between lovers or what?"

Domino shook her head. "Neither,"

Andy was confused. "I don't understand."

Domino thought for a moment. "I'm celibate."

Andy was stupefied. "What?"

"I'm experimenting with celibacy for the last three years, and I've never felt better," Domino confirmed.

"But doing what you do, don't you feel the urge?" Andy asked.

"I told you I stopped doing it," Domino reminded him.

"Ah yes," Andy said laughing.

Domino placed her purse on her knees. "I should be home working on my paper."

Andy was curious. "What paper?"

"I'm writing my final for my master's," Domino said.

"That's wonderful, what is about?" Andy asked.

"It's about Doctors," Domino shrugged.

"Doctors, are you're kidding me?"

"It's a very serious problem and nobody knows about it," Domino declared.

"What's wrong with them?"

"Doctors are just like you and I, but their profession keeps us function. A lot of them are toying with their patients, and make ridiculous assumptions. They degrading remarks during an operation is a perfect example," Domino stated.

Andy was shocked. "My doctors better respect me or I will stop visiting them."

"How often do you see your doctors?"

"I don't like to be sick," Andy quipped. "And only see them when it's absolutely necessary."

"That's the problem," Domino stated. "People see their doctors in a nauseous state, and behave differently."

"That's obvious."

"Doctors postulate their opinions based on the miserable creatures they observe, and their subconscious assumptions remain long after the patient is cured," Domino explained.

Andy was startled. "I've never thought of that."

"Doctors are like everybody else," Domino continued. "Their diagnoses can be influenced by their race, their prejudice, or religious believes. Not counting the phobias they have."

Andy was astonished. "But don't they take an oath to treat everyone equally?"

"Are you talking about the Hippocratic Oath?" Domino stated.

Andy nodded. "Yes, I think they swear an oath Jupiter."

Domino shook her head and corrected him. "They swear to Apollo, but don't you think it's a bit out dated?

Andy chuckled. "It's a tradition."

"Believe me," Domino continued. "There are doctors out there who think the field of medicine is the sadistic assholes paradise. I won't be surprised if the greatest mass murder in history would turn out to be a doctor, with a help from his nurse."

Andy doubted her statement. "Why it always has to be a man and not a woman?"

"History is filled with strong woman's scorns," Domino stated. "But in real life women are under constant pressure and intimidation."

"I think it's their motherly love, God blessed them with."

"Andrew, will you please leave God out of it?" Domino cried.

Andy was unwavering. "Why should I?"

Domino shrugged, drumming her purse with her fingers. "Because illusion and reality won't mix, and lots of women get shafted in the name of God…. Well, it was nice talking to you," Domino said, extending her hand.

"It was my pleasure," Andy said, getting out of his chair and shaking her hand.

"By the way how's your kitty?" Domino asked, pulling her hand away.

"She still has a bad eye and people tell me I should have her spayed," Andy replied.

"You should do it, or the horny bitch will drive you nuts?" Domino said, and left.

CHAPTER 19

Andy was driving in a semi hypnotic state, envisioning Domino's back sway under the short, dove gray jacket, and had to force the picture from his mind if he wanted to get home in one piece. He stopped to buy groceries and standing in the checkout lane he heard people talk about poor old Frank, and his huge family. Andy stopped at Dana's Drug Store to pick up a prescription and when he got home, Cilla was waiting for him by the door.

When Andy unpacked the groceries he threw the brown paper bag on the living room floor, and watched Cilla run in and out of it. He made tea and with tea mug in hand Andy stopped by the bookcase and pulled out the door, of course it was empty. He pushed it back and went to the couch, watching the cat play with the paper bag. Andy swirled his brew and wished there was a joint to go with it.

Cilla got tired playing and now was grooming herself. "What am I going to do with you?" Andy asked. "You come in my life without a warning label?"

When Andy let Cilla in the house he was sure he can handle the damned cat without any difficulties, not knowing the cuddly kitty can scratch and bite. Now Andy was questioning his abilities and wondered if he would have been successful without Dorothy. Every problem Andy faced he discussed it with her, and now that she has gone Andy was lost. With Dorothy, even the muddiest ideas became crystal clear, and he missed her so much. He didn't feel whole because the two of them were always one.

Sipping his brew from the tea-mug, Andy remembered the time when they visited Italy and spent a few days on the island of Capri. One evening they had a candlelight dinner on the shore in a romantic setting, and he told Dottie how much he admired her sense of beauty. Andy could never forget the appreciative look in her eyes, and wanted to tell her that he also loved her logical mind, but revealing his deep appreciation of her intellect somehow hold him. Now it was too late, and Andy knew that he missed out on something wonderful.

Swirling his drink Andy stared in the air then lifted his glass and gulped its content. He went to fix another one but decided to have something stronger. Andy poured a glass of scotch, and back in the living room he placed his glass on the coffee table. Leaning back into the soft leather of his couch, Andy knew that Dorothy's memory will remain with him for the rest of his life, but begin to realize its intensity and wondered if he can get lost in it. The thought that he can be lost in the past and won't be able to return into the present bothered him, and Andy wanted the idea vanish from his mind. He placed his drink on the table, rubbed his chest and arms, then went to his computer and typed in cats.

Andy learned about cats as much as he was able to stomach, and the traumatic procedure of spaying almost made him sick. But there was no other alternative and he looked for animal hospitals. He found one called Gateway in his old neighborhood on Los Feliz Boulevard, and it made Andy reminisce of the good old days. His parents wanted him to learn about life and through their connections his father got him a summer job as a tour guide at Universal Studios Tours. He found him a bachelor's pad in the Rancho, on Los Feliz Boulevard, and bought him a Porsche. After all the years, whenever Andy drove by he noticed the changes, but remembered the pleasant memories. He recalled playing golf on the short course next to the LA River, and the train rides he took from the Atwater Village Train Station, to the Del Mar Race Track.

Staring at the hospitals logo on the computer screen Andy felt good about his choice and knew, Cilla will be safe there.

The following morning Andy woke up with a slight hangover, and walked around with it till it became unbearable. Not knowing what to do Andy decided to give Sam a call, and ask his advice.

"So, you did like the joint," Sam chuckled.

"How the hell would you know that?" Andy asked.

"They all call when they run out of the stuff," Sam answered.

"Damn it Sam, you sound like a pusher."

"A pusher told me that," Sam chortled.

The two of them had a few more laughs and then Sam told Andy to get a physician's recommendation and take the document to the nearest weed store to buy the stuff. Sam also suggested a good looking woman for company, and Andy almost mentioned Domino. After they hung up, Sam e-mailed Andy the addresses of a few cannabis distributers in his area, with a weed doctor's address. Since Andy had nothing else to do, he went to see the doctor and claimed sleep disorder. In no time Andy was out the door with the blessed note. He found a cannabis distributer and when he walked in there were at least two uniformed guards with guns, and he had to identify himself with his driver's license. Andy filled out the paperwork and was able to enter the inner sanctum through a secured door. When he asked about the marihuana leafs he found out it's just a symbol, and if you try to buy to smoke them they would think you're nuts. A good looking young woman explained the variety of strains, and Andy learned about indica, sativa and the hybrids. He wound up with a good size plastic jar filled with Blue Dream, and being a first time customer they also gave him a bunch of freebies.

Driving home Andy stopped on a red light, and his heart skipped a bit when a police car pulled up next to him and the officer check him out. Less than thirty years ago if they would have found on him the amount of drugs he just bought legally, he would be laying on the ground handcuffed with at least five cops kneeling on him, and in court the Judge would have thrown the book at him. When the light turned green Andy smiled, and gently stepped on the accelerator.

At home, Andy opened the package on the kitchen table and examined them. There was a machine rolled joint, a chip wood bud crusher, a small glass pipe, rolling paper, some candy and a cheap lighter.

Andy rolled the joint between his fingers and pulled its length under his nose. He placed it on a porcelain saucer, and to enjoy his first free and legal joint in Los Angeles, California, Andy prepared himself for the occasion. He heated water for his tea and threw the rest of the cannabis into the bookcase door. He changed into his lung outfit, and put on his silk, chines robe with the dragon on the back. In the kitchen Andy opened the window, and outside on the crooked tree the squirrels were chasing each other. An airliner flew overhead to land on Bob Hope Airport less than five miles away and Andy inhaled the fresh air, wormed by the California sun.

Andy washed and dried a lemon and after cutting it in half, he immediately washed the acid off the knife. When the kettle whistled Andy poured the hot water on the teabag in the mug and left enough room for the goodies. He dipped the teabag in the hot water twenty four times, once for every hour of the day and then squeezed in the lemon juice, poured in one teaspoon of Manuka honey and topped it with spiced rum.

At the kitchen table Andy tasted his brew then lit the joint. He held his breath then blown the smoke out through the open window. Under the influence of the cannabis, Andy's mind filled with a liberated feeling, and pushing his chair away he placed his heels on the table.

Andy thought that smoking buds and not leaves must be a step in the right direction, and relished his mental state. He was enjoying his unplugged mind, when some harsh words sipped through the window. When Andy peeked out he saw the woman from upstairs with her husband, sniffing the air.

"This is terrible, the stench is all over the place," she complained.

"I'm not putting up with this, I'm calling the police," her husband said it indignantly.

The man must have had his speaker phone on, because Andy heard the phone ring, and the dispatcher's answer. "This is the emergency hotline, may I help you."

"I would like to report drug use in my apartment building."

"What kind of drugs are you talking about?" Andy heard the dispatcher's voice.

"He's smoking marihuana, and the air is filled with it," Andy's neighbor stated.

"Sir, cannabis use is legal in California."

"But I can smell it right here on the street."

"Is he smokes it out on the street?"

"He's inside his apartment, blowing the smoke out the window," Andy heard, and puffed some more smoke out. "He just did it again," the guy whined, and Andy snickered.

"You can knock on his door and ask him to stop doing it," the dispatcher advised.

Andy's neighbor was obstinate. "What if he refuses?"

The voice on the phone was calm. "Sorry sir, we can't do anything else."

But Andy's neighbor was unwavering. "Can you send out a police to investigate?"

"The police department has important things to attend to," the voice said, and the phone went dead.

"You heard it, the police sided with him," the man complained.

"With a drug using criminal," his wife declared, and Andy blow some more smoke out.

"This is the kind of people we have to put up with. No class, no class at all," Andy's neighbor declared, and they left.

Andy reached down and stroked the cat. "Now we are even with them."

CHAPTER 20

When Andy called the animal hospital a recorded message instructed the listeners how to prepare their pets for the procedure. It was so simple that he was pissed for not calling them earlier. Andy decided to take Cilla to the pet hospital the very next morning, and knowing what she will go through, Andy treated her extra special. He placed out treats and changed her drinking water at least four times, stroking her constantly. About eight o'clock in the evening Andy threw out the remaining food and water washed the dishes and was getting Cilla ready for her big day. The next morning Cilla fallowed Andy around crying and wanting her food and water, but Andy was adamant. He learned how to be cruel in the Universal Studios black tower.

When the time came to take Cilla to the animal hospital Andy unceremoniously shoved her in the bag. He was careful, but every time he bumped the carrying case into something Cilla moaned. Andy placed the carrying case in the car's passenger floor and pulled his hand across the screen. On the road Andy watched his driving because he was not alone, and got off the freeway at the Los Feliz exit turning east. Just after the railroad tunnel on Los Feliz Boulevard, Andy found the address and pulled into their parking lot.

The waiting room was filled with people and their pets, and at the desk Andy pulled ticket number 37. He took a seat and when his number was called a nurse ushered him into a white examination room. Andy placed the carrying case on the table and unzipped one end, and Cilla came out looking around. A knock on the door scared her and she rushed back into the bag. The veterinarian came in wearing white, and shook Andy's hand. He removed Cilla from the carrying case to be examined.

"She's to be neutered," Andy said and the vet corrected him.

"She is to be spayed

"Oh yes, spayed," Andy stuttered.

The veterinarian examined Cilla's bad eye and said. "It looks bad."

"Can it be fixed?" Andy asked.

The doctor looked at the eye one more time and said. "That won't be a problem."

"How much will it cost?" Andy asked.

"No more than fifty bucks," the doctor said.

"Just do it," Andy blurted.

Andy was so excited he didn't even remember living the place, and found himself standing on the curb waiting for a car go by on the dead end street. His heart was racing and the beam on his face was so notched in, not even a boxer could have pummeled it off.

Eventually Andy realized what he was doing when he tried to open the car's door with his apartment key. With outstretched arms Andy leaned against his car and inhaled twenty four times. When he finally was inside Andy leaned back in the leather seat and looked up, but the moon roof was closed. Andy started the engine, opened the moon roof, switched to a Jazz station and glided from the parking lot blasting Count Base's, The Kidd from Red Bank.

Driving home Andy felt so elated he didn't even mind the way people drive, and cheerfully went around the slow drivers. He stopped to have breakfast at Tallyrand, read the newspaper and solved the daily Sudoku with ease. When Andy got home he felt good just by walking around the house, not having a damned cat to worry about. He turned on the TV but the news was filled with misguided people killing each other for their misguided believes, and the shows were filled with sex and violence. Andy turned the TV off, changed into his gym wear and drove to Griffith Park. He was in the middle of his walk when Andy realized that he was in the neighborhood earlier, and if he would have planned his day the stroll would be over by now.

With Dottie they scheduled everything sometimes years ahead, and they never had to worry about having a cat interfering with their lives. Suddenly a thought occurred to him and it was so intense Andy stopped, and the runner behind him had to change lane. He always knew that Dottie run the house, planned everything and he was nothing more than a useless bystander, trying to stay out of her way. By the time Andy reached the end of the road where it turns around the golf course, he felt totally useless and was in a pathetic state of mind.

Holding on to the railing Andy spit over it once to the left, and once to the right. Andy inhaled deeply and widely circling his arms, he watched a golfer miss his put. Andy wondered if he had anything to do with it because even though the golfer was far away, they made eye contact.

Further down the road Andy glanced at his watch when a golf ball hit a tree, and flew over the fence. The white golf ball with red polka dots rolled right affront of him, and Andy picked it up. When the guy came to look for his golf ball Andy reached in his pocket to give it back, but recognized the guy from earlier and kept on going.

Andy was thinking of the golfer when he stepped over an ant, and when he looked up he saw one of the lords of Griffith Park, scratching himself next to the flagpole on the putting green. The coyote may have looked relaxed but was aware of him going by. To the beast Andy was just food but as long as there was easier feasts around he was safe. The park was a paradise for the healthy beast, and the coyote's main concern was not getting food but being one. A cougar named P22, was hanging around the Los Feliz area, and if the coyote was able to stay away the park was his to roam.

There was a fence between them but Andy tensed as he walked by staring at the coyote, and hoping he knows the rules. Andy was thinking about all the wild animals around the park and recalled the time when he wanted to leave Cilla out here. Just the thought of doing it made him cringe, and was glad that she was in the hospital, safe under a surgeon's scalpel.

When Andy reached the parking lot he glanced at his watch. He covered the last mile in seventeen and a half minutes, instead of his casual twenty. Andy took a deep breath before he opened the car door, and took another one when he saw all the bird shit covering the car seats.

Andy patiently removed a roll of paper towel from the trunk, cleaned up the mass and discarded the used towels into a trashcan. Andy placed the remaining paper roll in the trunk, and reached in his pocket for the golf ball with the red dots. After a short scrutiny Andy tossed it in a tray with the others, and closed the trunk. When he was in the driver's seat Andy started the engine and closed the moon roof.

CHAPTER 21

When Andy got home and opened the door, he was careful not to let the cat out even though he knew Cilla was in the hospital. Getting out of his running outfit, Andy tried to make sense of his mental state but it was too complicated and decided to take a shower.

Andy was soaping himself and was singing La Donna e mobile from Rigoletto, when suddenly the water turned cold and he had to wash the soap off with ice cold water. "The curse of apartment living," Andy mumbled, drying himself, feeling invigorated.

Coming from the bathroom Andy saw Cilla run by and turned her head to look at him. They made eye contact and going around the corner she disappeared. Andy shook his head in disbelieve, the cat was in the hospital but the illusion was so real Andy checked the living room, the bedroom, and even looked under the bed.

At the kitchen table Andy rolled a joint and lit up, acknowledging the fact that he was accustomed to visualize Dorothy, but never a damned cat. He inhaled deeply and was holding his breath when the phone ring and Andy blew the smoke out. "Yeah, it's me," Andy answered

"This is Gateway animal hospital. We would like you to know, the operation was a success."

"What about the eye?" Andy blurted.

"They only told me that everything is fine, and you can pick her up tomorrow after eight AM in the morning," the pleasant voice said cheerfully.

"Thank you, thank you very much," Andy said with a sniff, trying to see the wall clock through his clouds of tears. It was 1 PM.

"Poor, poor thing," Andy sniffed

He felt for Cilla, she was in a cage somewhere hopefully asleep and not aware of it. Lighting a new joint, Andy leaned back and placed his legs up on the kitchen table. He took a hit and was trying to blow the smoke out like Sam did, of course he couldn't but it reminded him to give him a call. Andy placed the joint on the saucer, went to get his phone and dialed the number, he light the joint again then hit the green button.

"Well, hello Andrew," Sam said.

Andy was surprised. "How do you know it was me?"

"Your name was on the phone," Sam laughed.

Andy was amused. "I had that gadget in my office but not at home."

"Do you have a cell phone?" Sam asked.

"I'm talking to you on one right now," Andy stated.

"Then learn how to use it."

"What makes you think I don't know how to use a cell phone?

"Never mind how did you like the stuff?"

"Sam, I did exactly what you told me and it worked. The doctor gave me the recommendation, I bought the stuff and now I'm stoned."

"You're not alone bro, you're not alone."

"Man, that place is like a candy store, for grownups."

"Yeah, they sure have a lot of stuff. What did you get?"

"I got Blue Dream."

"Blue Dream is good."

"You smoked it?"

"Of course, it's very popular."

"They've had Sour Diesel, Gorilla Glue, and a bunch of other crazy names."

"Yeah, they have the stuff to get you into the mood you want."

"They have things to place you in the mood?" Andy asked.

"Oh yeah, I'm waiting for the one that would help me put up with my mother in law," Sam said with a hearty laughter and Andy joined in.

"Are they in town?" Andy asked.

"Yeah, they are staying with us, you know the wedding."

"No, I don't. What kind of wedding?"

"Raymond is getting married and it's going to be next weekend. Didn't you get the invitation?"

"Damn it, I forgot to check my mail."

"We sent them out, two weeks ago."

"Are you're kidding me?"

"How can I kid you, my son is getting married."

"Sorry, I was thinking about something else. Sam, I know you're busy but I would like to see Ray before the wedding."

"Come by next Wednesday, we'll have a small gathering and Ray be here."

"Thanks Sam."

"I want you to be careful with that stuff; you're not used to it."

"I only smoke it when I'm home."

"Good, than I see you next Wednesday."

"Yeah, see you Wednesday," Andy said, hanging up and went out to check his mail.

Later in the day, Andy had four more visions of the cat and once when he was watching television, he thought Cilla went by and rubbed herself to his legs. Andy knew his mind was playing tricks on him but this time, he was able to blame the cannabis.

It was about ten at night when the day's activities finally cut up with him and he became very sleepy. Andy had a hard time concentrating and didn't know what he was watching. He turned the TV off, and slipping on the couch was out of the question, Andy gathered all his strength to stagger into bed. As soon as he was under the cover his day came to an end, and his dreams begin.

Andy was walking Cilla in Griffith Park, and watched the dust rise as she hit the ground with her powerful paws. The cat proudly strolled in the center of the road and was pulling Andy on the tight leash. With her tail up, she was hissing at the dogs going by with their tails between their legs, and Andy was thinking.

"Where are the coyotes now?"

CHAPTER 22

Coming from his bedroom Andy yawned and looked around, finding the place strange without the cat. It took him a while to realize that walking the cat in Griffith Park was a dream, and Cilla was in the hospital.

Andy was about to get into his workout gear when he glanced at the wall clock and it showed seven AM. It was too late to do his daily routines and Andy had to control himself not to get irritated on the day when Cilla was coming home from the hospital. He had no other choice but to hold his breath, count up to twenty four, and take a shower.

This time he was lucky, and the water was nice and worm from the beginning to the end. Andy dried himself and looked in the fogged up mirror, holding a small belly flab. It felt like he lost about five pounds, but somehow he still had at least five more pounds to go. After he got his khakis and polo shirt on, Andy pushed his foot into his slip-ons without the socks, and went to the kitchen. He washed the floor and when he was done Andy opened a fresh can of whitefish fillets, and poured its content on a shiny tray. He refilled the dish with filtered water, and looked around with a satisfied nod.

On the 135 Freeway Andy got into the second lane that led to Interstate 5, and exited on Los Feliz going east. He reached the hospital before it opened, and he patiently stayed in line. About five minutes later the doors opened, and he was the last one to enter.

In the lobby Andy patiently waited his turn, and his heart jumped when the bill included the eye drops. He paid the bill with his credit card and this time he really didn't care how much they charged.

When the nurse handed him the carrying case, Andy felt from the weight that Cilla was inside. With the case hanging from his shoulder Andy was holding the paper bag with the eye drops, and carefully went through the exit. He looked left and right before he crossed the dead end street, and went to the passenger's side of his car, and opened the door. Andy placed the carrying case on the seat and unzipped one end. Cilla was laying there with a plastic cone on her head, and she looked at Andy with those sad, but beautiful eyes.

Andy smiled, sniffed and wiped his eyes with the back of his hands. He was able to see the left eye was only half the size of the right one, and not as bright. He reached in to take her out and hug her, but she cried out and Andy remembered the other operation.

"You poor thing," Andy said, zipping up the bag and carefully placing it on the floor.

Wiping his eyes with Starbuck napkins Andy inhaled a few more times, and then started the engine. He turned off the radio and carefully drove from the parking lot with his precious cargo. When Andy got on the freeway he drove slow in the slow lane, and stopped looking into the rearview mirror to see how many cars are piled up behind him.

When Andy finally made it home he pulled into his parking place and turned off the engine. Andy was thinking about lifting the case over the gear shift but changed his mind, and went around the car to the passenger's side and gently removed the carrying case. Making sure it was constantly level, Andy reached his apartment and went straight in the kitchen. He placed the carrying case on the floor, and checked the food and water one more time. Andy saw his footprint on the floor, and tore off some paper towels to wipe it clean. When everything looked perfect Andy unzipped the carrying case. He was waiting for Cilla to show herself but she took her time. Andy pulled out his chair and waited, till Cilla poked her head out with that plastic cone on her head. When she came out of the carrying bag Andy picked her up and placed her across his lap. He turned her over and saw the shaved stomach with the long scar. The wound was already healing, but it made her look very fragile.

"Very soon the treads can be removed," Andy thought, and was glad that Cilla was a healthy cat. And now with her eye fixed, she was on her way to become a beautiful princess. Andy gently stroked her, and was surprised when she cried out. He placed Cilla on the floor, and she looked up at him with those beautiful eyes and timidly minnow.

Walking around with the plastic cone on her head, Cilla behaved like a born trouper. She ate a little, drink some water and then disappeared. Andy knew she went to sleep somewhere and postponed his noisy chores.

Late in the evening Andy turned off the TV and picked up a book called War and Peace, by Leo Tolstoy. He promised Dorothy on her death bed that he will spend the rest of his life reading it, but soon after he opened the book he stopped. Everything he read was familiar, because he already saw the movie. Andy blew the dust off the book, and placed it back on the coffee table.

CHAPTER 23

It was late in the morning and Andy checked the usual hiding places, but Cilla was nowhere to be found. "Where can a cat hide with a plastic cone on her head?"

Andy washed her dish then opened a can of cat food, when Cilla strolled in the kitchen with the cone on her head. Shoving a portion of cat food from the can on to Cilla's tray, Andy glanced at her sitting on the floor and couldn't help but smile. Her shaved chest with the stiches was visible, and when Andy looked into those eyes there was trust in them. Cilla was such a pretty sight Andy got his cellphone and took a few pictures of her. When he replayed them Cilla looked great on every photo. Andy closed his eyes and to his surprise Cilla also closed hers, and like a little girl she shyly turned away.

Andy put the phone away and picked up the Lysine bottle, dropped a 500 Milligram Lysine capsule in his hand, pulled it apart and mixed its content into the cat food. "Come and get it," Andy whispered placing the dish on the floor. And for the first time since she left the hospital, Cilla lifted her tail.

Andy slumped in a chair watching Cilla eat, and couldn't help but wonder how the hell did she slept with that damned cone?

Cilla was truly amazing and carried her burden with dignity, like she learned it in her previous lives. "I wonder if they believe in God," Andy mused knowing how loving Cilla was. If God is the good in all of us then Cilla have a lot of God in her. She always wants attention but also try to please, and when Cilla does something wrong she feels bad and hides.

Andy was thinking about all the other animals of the world, planted into paradise by God. He learned from watching the National Geography Specials that every wild animal is a loving parent, and ready to defend their families with their own lives. Andy believed that when you experience love, it is enough to be God's children. It was almost inconceivable to believe that intelligent people like Raymond cannot understand such a simple thing. Andy loved Raymond like he would have loved his own son, and now that he is grown up and was getting married Andy didn't want him to have a cold and Godless life. Knowing he's going to see Raymond later in the day, Andy didn't know how he's going to approach his atheistic believes and decided to do it by ear.

Andy knew Raymond all his life, he just couldn't figure out when he's gone wrong. Andy didn't spend the last five years reading War and Peace, but somehow time just went by and things gone wrong.

Andy decided to roll a joint, and when it was done he removed a porcelain saucer from the dish rack, and noticed the Navaho motives. The saucer was from his mother's favorite set of dinnerware and Andy remembered when he got into a tantrum for not getting something, and wanted to break a Navaho dish. As it turned out the Navaho dish-set was the only one left intact in his heirloom. Andy held up the saucer and appreciated the simple, elegant lines and couldn't help but wonder what the Navaho had in his peace pipe?

Andy placed the saucer and the joint back on the table, and admired them as the two went so well together. Knowing that Cilla can't jump up on the table with the cone on her neck, Andy went in the bathroom to brush his teeth when he remembered cone or no cone, Cilla can jump. With the brush in his mouth Andy rushed back in the kitchen and passed Cilla with her burden. In the kitchen Andy placed the joint in the plastic tube and left it on the saucer.

Taking a shower Andy was hoping he won't feel guilty for skipping his walk in Griffith Park, because he already felt terrible for not knowing what to say to Raymond. After he dried himself Andy placed his foot on the toilet seat and cut his toenails, constantly thinking of Raymond. He believed that he will be able to bring him back to Christ with kindness and understanding after all he was Raymond's God father.

The rest of the morning went fast and before he left, Andy made sure Cilla had enough food and water. He picked up the joint from the Navaho saucer and placed it in his shirt's pocket. Andy made reservation for lunch at The Smoke House, so he checked himself in the mirror and when he saw the joint showed in his shirt pocket, he put a jacket on. The food in the restaurant was great and knowing he has to drive, Andy only tasted his wine. On the freeway he got into the fast lane and cruised all the way to the Lake Avenue exit, where he encountered some traffic going south.

Slowly turning onto Sam's driveway, Andy enjoyed the sound of the white marble gravel under the tiers, and when he drove into the circular driveway he saw at least ten cars in the paved parking lot. Entering the marble he wanted to ask the man at the door in his fake Indian costume with tall green, red and yellow feathers on his head, what is going on but he only opened the door. Andy looked around the stone cold place with worm holes, the only building in the world as soon as he stepped in, he wanted to get out.

People were rushing around and Andy had to watch out not to bump into them. They were mostly woman but some of them were men, and they openly looked him over. He almost made it to the back door when Dolores saw him.

"Andrew darling, it's so nice to see you," Dolores said, holding both sides of her cheek for the phony kisses. "I can't talk now. You can find Sam in his hiding place."

"What's going on?"

"It's the wedding dress, and I hired Lorenzo to fix it."

"Ah, I see. Well, good luck."

When Andy made it to the back door he burst through it and inhaled, trying to get rid of his allergy of the building. By the time he got to Sam's bungalow Andy was breading freely, but when he opened the door the fumes from inside hit him in the face.

"How could you live like this?" Andy grumbled, pumping the door before he closed it.

"I know it's a mass," Sam said, grabbing Andy's hand and bumping his shoulder into his.

"I'm not talking about the mass I'm talking about the air?"

"You right I should turn on the fan," Sam said, getting back in his chair.

"Don't you like fresh air?"

"Of course I do, there's plenty of it outside."

"Ah, never mind."

"Care to have one of this?" Sam said lifting an ornate box, filled with pre rolled joints.

"No thanks," Andy said, reaching in his shirt pocket and proudly removing from the plastic tube his joint, twisted on both ends. Andy flipped his Bic lighter and lit up, and then holding his breath he coughed the smoke out. "What's wrong with the dress?"

"She's pregnant and keeps growing out of it," Sam snickered.

"That's not funny," Andy guffawed.

"I told them the baby will be out before the wedding, but they hushed me off."

"They won't believe you?"

"They know I'm right, it's my wife Didi. She wants the wedding before the baby comes."

"Why they waited for the last moment?" Andy asked.

"It's been going on for quite a while," Sam grumbled.

"How's Ray taking it?"

"He's okay. Ray has my temperament otherwise he would have had a nervous breakdown by now."

"Where is he?"

"He's with them," Sam said, reaching for his pipe, and was lighting it when the door opened and Ray walked in. He was a tall, good looking kid and being six foot nine, when he turned sideways he looked like a telephone pole with a round thing on the top.

Without looking around Ray took the glass pipe from his father and took an urgent puff. Andy watched the ember brightens in the glass pipe, burning its way into the buds. Blowing the smoke out, Raymond noticed his father's nod and turned to fallow his gaze.

"Uncle Andy," Ray said with a respectfully surprise. With smoke coming out of his mouth, he handed his father the glass pipe and shook hands with Andy, and they hugged.

"Raymond, you look great," Andy said looking up at him.

"I wish I could feel that way," Ray said, reaching for his dad's pipe again.

"What's going on?" Sam asked.

"I tried to talk sense to them but they won't listen."

"Don't let the women bother you," Sam stated.

"Mother is the worst she's just thrown me out."

"How's the dress?" Andy asked.

"This time they expend it so much around her waist it looks like a miniskirt on front, with a long train in the back."

"Why don't you get some more material?" Andy asked.

Sam shook his head. "The dress is one of those only ones."

"Then cut it from the trail?" Andy suggested.

"I tried to tell them that when they pushed me out," Raymond moaned.

"Don't tell them anything, let the women figure it out," Sam shouted. Raymond looked at his father questioningly, and Sam continued with disgust. "They are women, all of them."

"You're so right," Raymond nodded and winked at Andy. "Let them figure it out."

"The main thing is you're here and now you can relax," Sam said, taking his chair, and then turning to Andy he asked. "Where were we?"

"I don't remember." Andy said, watching Ray taking a pre rolled cannabis from the box.

"What are you staring at?" Ray said to Andy with a bit of irritation, lighting the joint.

"I've never seen you smoking marihuana before," Andy smirked.

"I've never seen you smoke one either."

"I gave it up, long before you were born," Andy said lighting his, and taking a hit.

"I heard you guys used to smoke the leaves?" Ray laughed.

"It's true," Sam snickered. "I used to smoke Humble County Purple."

"Sam, didn't they call marihuana the gateway drug?" Andy asked.

"You mean the gateway for stronger drugs?" Ray asked.

"Yes," Andy stated.

"Some people will always want more than just a buzz." Sam said, lifting his pipe.

"Have you ever used stronger drugs?" Ray asked his father.

"When you in the major leagues you always want to improve. I can never forget this famous baseball player who told me that he never left the dugout without snorting cocaine, so I tried."

"Did it help?" Ray asked.

"I thought it did."

"Have it really?" Ray inquired.

"It did not, and the trouble with cocaine the more you sniff the more you want."

"So what happened?" Raymond probed his father.

"One day they called me in the office and showed me some tapes, and then the coach wanted to know the reason for my decline."

"What did you tell him?" Ray inquired.

"I told him that I was using cocaine."

"You told him you were using cocaine?" Ray said to his father with admiration.

"Yes. He helped me to get off of it, and we became best of friends," Sam chuckled.

"I thought I was your best friend?" Andy uttered.

"You're family," Sam grinned.

Raymond stood up. "Who wants a beer?"

"Good idea," Sam said.

Andy nodded and when Raymond left he turned to Sam and whispered. "He handles himself so well."

"Oh yeah," Sam nodded.

The two of them smiled at each other and then patiently waited for Ray to hand out the cans.

Ray popped his can open and turned to Andy. "So how's Mister Hayym doing?"

Sam was bewildered. "Who is mister Hayym?"

"When I was in high school I had a part in a stupid play some kid wrote," Andy said. "And I played Hayym a Jewish ruffian from the Bronx. The story was copied after Sinbad the sailor stuck on land, and you can get sea sick just by reading the script."

"I never heard of that one, you're not even Jewish," Sam said, shaking with laughter.

"We all done stupid things," Andy said.

"You're so right, I was always in trouble," Sam chortled.

"I deed had my share," Andy chuckled.

"Didn't you guys learned by now?" Raymond asked.

"Life is full of surprises, and if you don't know what you're doing it can pile up," Sam declared.

"And you really hate yourself when you repeat them," Andy added, turning to Ray. "May I ask you something?"

"Shoot," Ray said.

"Why you waited so long to get married?" Andy asked.

"We never wanted the wedding," Ray replied.

Andy was flabbergasted. "Don't you love her?"

"Of course I do, we just don't believe in marriage."

"Don't you believe in the sanctity of marriage?"

"We do believe in the sanctity, without the rituals. We are atheists." Raymond stated.

"When Sam told me that, I couldn't believe it."

"Leave me out of it," Sam said.

"How could you turn your back on God?" Andy said lighting Ray's joint.

"I can't turn my back on something that doesn't exist."

"I know you're smarter than that."

"Not really the more I learn the dumber I feel, and God has nothing to do with it."

"Have ever occurred to you that God will test your faith in him?"

"I told you that God has nothing to do with my life. Okay?"

"Everything we do is by God's grace."

"Uncle Andy, can we talk about something else. You're giving me a headache."

"You're talking about headaches when I'm trying to save your immortal soul?"

"There are many other things we can talk about."

"Raymond, there's nothing more important than your immortal soul."

"I can think of at least ten, right now."

"Raymond, this is not a joke. How could you do this to your father?"

"I told you to leave me out of it," Sam barked.

"If you don't believe in a God, where are you going to found your moral guidance?"

"In a civilized society, the laws of the Gods are replaced by the laws of men."

"I'm talking about the one and only God."

"Uncle Andy, our addictive nature enjoys a lot of other things besides drugs and alcohol and your God is one of them," Ray stated.

"How could you make such a mistake, faith in God is the cure." Andy said calmly.

"The mistake is yours Uncle Andy," Raymond declared. "Existence is spiritual and we do need spiritual guidance. But not leadership from a bunch of morons, who think a prayer to a nonexistent deity, will help."

"Ray, I'm not talking about addictions or creasy believes. I'm talking about basic human values you can only get from God."

"Uncle Andy, our morals were distorted by religious leaders to benefit themselves."

"There's a lot of truth in it, but you can't deny God."

"Uncle Andy, religion is a self-induced mental disease and I don't want to talk about it."

"What you are saying is sacrilege."

Raymond finished his beer and crushed the can. "I'm tired, and would like to change the subject."

Sam enjoyed watching the two and considered Andy one of his friends, just didn't know if he was the one who influenced Raymond about giving up basketball.

"Okay, if you're an atheist then why the fuss about the white dress?" Andy asked.

"It has nothing to do with Ray, it's my wife Dolores. She's very religious."

"Dad built a chapel for her, its right behind us with the six foot glass cross on the door."

"Most Latinos are religious. God bless them." Andy stressed.

"And Didi is the living proof of that," Sam proclaimed. "When she found out about the pregnancy, she immediately demanded a church wedding and wanted the bride to wear a white dress."

"But white represent virginity," Andy laughed.

"Yes I know," Ray snickered.

Andy shook his head. "Why would do something like that?"

Sam chuckled. "I live with that woman for more than twenty five years, and sometimes I just can't figure her out."

"How come I never had that problem?" Andy thought thinking of Dorothy, when the door opened and Eric, the Rock and Roll playing long haired freak from England walked in. Andy sold his house to the man and ever since that day he couldn't stand the sight of him. With his shoulder long dyed blond hair and his tight fitting clothes, the fifty some year old Eric looked like a bad memory. But his music was making him millions.

"You're all busted," Eric said laughing, shaking hands with Sam and Raymond, and when he saw Andy he grinned. "Look who's here, my greatest benefactor in the colonies. Mister Flowers, how are you doing Sir?"

"I'm doing just fine," Andy said, shaking hands with Eric.

"Do you know that your place, I mean my place, it almost doubled its value."

"Thanks for telling me," Andy said, getting back in his chair.

"Good think I run into you, where you get those English made door locks?"

"When my great grandfather built the house, he shipped it from England. You've had the same locks on your doors back home?"

"Oh no, we couldn't afford them, and I don't think they make them anymore. My father was a locksmith and I saw him installing in rich people's houses," Eric said on his way to the refrigerator. "Who wants a beer?"

Andy lifted his hand and Sam and Ray did the same.

"Now you have a house filled with those locks," Andy said.

"You meant my mansion?" Eric laughed, handing out the beer and opening his can.

"Yeah, your mansion," Andy mumbled from the side of his mouth.

"It is a beautiful place," Sam said to Andy.

"Yes I know," Andy shrugged. "I've grown up in it."

"And your old golf cart still works; I just used it coming here. Now we charge it with the new solar panels installed on the roof," Eric said, sinking in the remaining chair.

"You covered the sleight roof with solar panels?"

"Well, we couldn't cover it all, only the west and the south side. And do you remember the rose garden?"

Andy was astonished. "The entrance is on the south side, and you placed those things above the front door?"

"Yeah," Eric stated.

"What about the rose garden?" Andy asked in a hopeless tone. "Do you know those roses are award winning flowers?"

"No more. I dug them up and replace them with a beautiful, one hole golf course."

"You dug up the rose garden?"

"Yes, and believe me by the time I'm done with the place you won't recognize it."

"I believe you," Andy said, gulping his beer.

"Andy, you've never finished telling me what happened to the cat?" Sam asked, watching Andy crushing the beer can.

"You have a cat?" Ray asked.

"Well I'm not sure if it's mine. You see the cat came to my door just before Christmas, and I let it in for a night."

Eric scoffed. "The cat must love you. I can see the scratches and the bites."

"It's not that bad," Andy said, looking at his hands.

"You mean it was worse?" Erik jeered.

Not be able to come up with the right answer, Andy just stared at Eric.

"So, what happened to the cat's eye?" Sam asked.

"When I had her spayed they also scraped her eye," Andy said "And it only coast me fifty bucks."

"I'm glad, I can never forget the things you told me," Sam said with a straight face, but holding back laughter.

"Listen guys, I didn't know a damn thing about cats and she's been a very sweet kitty. She's alone in the world so what can I do?" Andy stated, watching Eric scratch his arms.

"You said the cat was black and white?" Sam asked.

"No it's gray and white," Andy said, taking his cellphone out and turning it on. When he found the picture of Cilla, Andy handed the cellphone to Sam.

"What a beautiful kitty, what's her name?" Sam asked.

"It's Cilla. Like Pris-Cilla," Andy emphasized.

"I can see Cilla's left eye is a lot smaller than the right one," Sam said, handing the phone to Ray.

"She's beautiful," Raymond stated. "And look at that mustache."

"She has a mustache?" Andy said, taking the phone from Ray, looking at the picture. "I don't see it."

"It is right there, can you see the white line above the lips?" Ray said, pointing it out.

"Well I'll be. As soon as I get home I'll check it out." Andy said handing the phone to Eric, but he pushed it away.

"I'm allergic to cats," Eric uttered.

"You're allergic to cats?" Andy said, pushing the phone with the cat's picture, close to Eric's face and he turned away.

"Get it away from me," Eric said, lifting his arms.

"Uncle Andy, why don't you keep it?" Ray asked.

"I'm really not a cat person, and I don't think I could handle the responsibility. Why don't you take it?" Andy said, turning to Eric.

"I hate cats," Eric said, scratching his hand.

"But look, she's beautiful," Andy said and shoved his I phone into Eric's face.

Eric turned his head and pushed the phone away. "Come on guys, cat's make me sick."

"If I would have known it, I would have brought the cat," Andy bantered.

"Uncle Andy, you've never seen my bride," Ray said, taking his I phone out. When he found the picture Ray handed the phone to Andy.

Andy pocketed his cellphone and took Ray's. He stared at the picture then holding it to his chest he said. "She's beautiful."

"Yes I know," Ray said reaching out to get his phone back, but Andy took one more look.

"What's her name?"

"Mellow, I mean Melody."

"What a nice name, Melody. She looks tall," Andy said, handing the phone back to Ray.

"Not really, she's about your height."

"Can I see it?" Eric asked.

Ray passed the phone to Eric. "You're a lucky man," he said, and handed the phone back.

"Every good man deserves a good woman." Andy said staring at Eric.

Sam noticed the tension between the two and interposed. "And she loves basketball."

"I'm glad," Andy said. "By the way what do you think of the Clippers?"

"The Clippers are a lousy team," Eric stated.

"I do watch the Clippers," Sam cuffed. "Every team goes through a period when nothing goes right. It's like a curse and there's not much can you do about it but ride it out."

"You think the Clippers are going through one right now?" Andy asked.

"Yes. It will take a lot of effort to get over it, and can break up the team."

Andy was in shock. "Break up the Clippers?"

"Yes, because the good players want to be successful and if they can't found it with the team they are with, they will go and seek it with another."

"Dad, you never won a ring and you were successful."

"I was a good player and signed great contracts," Sam stated. "But I'm paying for every major defeat."

"Well, somebody must win and somebody must loose. We saw you play and you were awesome," Andy stated.

"I've never seen Sam play," Eric said. "I didn't know who he was till he came over knocking on my door."

"I went over to shake his hand and he invited me in to smoke a joint. I knew it right then he's going to be a great neighbor," Sam said, with his typical laughter.

"You should have seen Sam play," Andy said to Eric. "He was truly great."

"I don't know anything about American games, I only watch football."

"You mean soccer," Andy snapped.

"No, it's foot-ball," Eric said, hitting his foot. "We kick the ball and if we touch it with our hands like you do, it's a penalty."

"Ah yes, you kick the ball and when you ketch up with it you kick it away again. It sounds very exciting. We have girls playing the game."

"There are strategies involved," Ray asserted.

"I know, I just don't like the game," Andy quipped, and winked.

"Then don't watch it," Eric said.

"I don't," Andy barked back with narrowed eyes.

"I have news for you," Sam smiled. "If they refuse to make American football games safer, the English one will replace it."

"It will never happen," Andy snapped.

"But dad, how could they make it safer?"

"Make it safer by removing the brutality and replace it with strategy," Sam affirmed.

"Then you have football," Eric laughed.

Andy was unwavering. "We watch a game to see a nice throw, a nice catch or a good block and the equipment should be designed to protect the players,"

"There's no protection against the body blow. It jiggles your body and scrambles the brain," Sam said, with a faraway stare.

"It also goes for football, when they use their heads to block the ball or head it in the net for a goal," Eric said.

"When you're active you're taking risks, and injuries are the way of life," Ray stated, thinking of his own injuries when he played basketball in high school and college.

"The trick is to go through each game without an injury," Andy supposed.

"It's not that easy, there are quite a few players who enjoy being rough," Sam smiled. "I had my eyes on some guys and they had their eyes on me."

"You purposely go out to hurt others?" Andy asked.

"We train to be tough, and sometimes it's scary," Sam stated.

"Were you ever afraid?" Ray asked.

"No, and even if I was I'll could never show it. In professional sports you build a reputation and your presence intimidates."

Ray disagreed. "Reputation only invites trouble."

"That's not the kind of reputation I'm talking about." Sam said. "The best athletes can avoid trouble with their behavior, and won't get hurt as often."

"Accidents happen no matter how good you are," Ray protested.

"Very true, but most of them are self-inflicted in the absence of discipline. The modern athlete must behave accordingly, on and off the field."

"Who do you think is the best athlete in the world today?" Andy asked.

"It's got to be Rodger Federer," Sam answered without hesitation.

"Dad I'm disappointed in you."

"Why would you?"

"I thought you're going to say Serena Williams."

"They are just great. I can never forget when Venus became a champion, and being black, she was a surprise. And then her father Richard declared that he had another one at home, a lot better."

"What about Usain Bolt?" Eric asked.

"He could be the greatest runner of all time," Sam answered. "He proved himself in three Olympics,"

Ray shook his head. "You all wrong, it's Mohamed Ali."

"I knew Ali when he was Cashes Clay, and saw him pay a heavy price for being the best in a brutal sport," Sam stated "I think he was a greater person than a champion."

"Okay then why did you choose Federer?" Andy asked, because he also liked Rodger.

"If you ever watch Federer play you know that tennis is not just hitting the ball back and forth," Sam said. "It's a mental game, and you can see the way Rodger over power his opponents with his cool behavior. And even when he loses it's not because he doesn't know how to play the game."

Eric nodded. "Yes, you right,"

Ray was indignant. "He knows how to please the crowd, but that don't qualify him to be the best sports figure in the world."

"I don't know if you noticed that all tennis players shake their legs when they are resting, but not Rodger," Sam explained. "He conserves his energy whenever he can, and Roger also pays attention to the game and not where he placed his water bottles."

"And Rodger doesn't get fired up to a game, he calms down to it," Andy added.

"Federer is an exemplary sports figure, but not the best in the world," Ray stated, finishing his beer.

"How come you didn't stay with basketball?" Eric inquired.

Andy was eager to hear what Ray is going to say. "Yes, why did you give up basketball?"

"I never gave up basketball, I still play."

"I meant professionally," Andy asked.

"Well, you had something to do with it."

Andy was surprised. "Me?"

"I should have known it was you, you backstabbing son of a bitch," Sam said flying out of his chair, but Ray was faster and blocked his father's path to Andy.

"What's going on?" Ray asked, holding on to his father.

"That son of a bitch talked you out of playing basketball," Sam pointed to Andy.

"I never, I always wanted him to be a basketball player," Andy said, standing up.

"You lying son of a bitch. If you wouldn't have talked him out of it, he would be playing someplace right now," Sam said, trying to get to Andy.

"Hold it Dad, it was my decision not his."

"Yes, after he talked you out of it."

"I would never do that!" Andy hollered back.

"I let you in my house and you stabbed me in the back. You're dead you hear me, you're dead!" Sam yelled.

Andy pushed out his chest. "Then come and kill me. I wanted him to play basketball more than you."

Staring at his father Raymond lifted his hand. "Just hold it. Don't you think I have something to say about it?"

Andy and Sam stared at each other, and Erik curled up on the big leather chair, trying to be invisible.

"I'm sorry if I became a disappointment," Raymond stated. "I never knew you had plans for me."

"I never had a plan for you. I just wanted you to be a good basketball player that's all, and then he came along." Sam pointed his chin at Andy.

"Nobody talked me out of anything," Raymond affirmed.

Andy was curious. "But you just said I've changed your mind, how the hell did I do that?"

"Do you remember our walks in Griffith Park?

"Yes of course, what about it?"

"It was just before graduation," Ray remembered. "It was the last time you went around the golf course because the smog from the freeway was bothering you."

"Oh yeah, go on," Andy recalled.

"You told me that freedom was the most important thing in your life."

"I told you that, not him," Sam exclaimed.

"You both told me that in your own ways."

"That's all?" Andy and Sam said it almost simultaneously, and then both turned to get back to their chairs.

"It doesn't mean you're not an asshole," Sam said, picking up his pipe.

"I never said I wasn't but you always been a lot better," Andy spit back.

"Who wants a beer?" Eric asked, jumping from his chair.

"I'm not in the mood," Sam mumbled, lighting his pipe.

"I want one," Ray said, looking at Andy and he nodded.

Andy was forlorn. "Raymond, basketball has nothing to do with freedom."

"Did you hear that?" Sam turned to his son.

"Dad, let me explain," Ray was collecting his thoughts. "You told me that I have to fight for freedom and defend it." Ray turned to Andy. "Uncle Andy, you told me that freedom should be free, like clean water or fresh air. "

"What does he know, my great grandfather was a slave and he had to fight to be free."

"This is interesting," Eric said handing out the beers.

"Don't you discuss freedom in your country, or you don't know what it is?" Andy asked.

"We have so much of it we are giving it away and don't discuss it at home," Eric jested.

"You could be right," Andy stated. "Freedom means deferent things to deferent people."

"But you told me freedom is universal and it's everybody's birth-right?" Ray spurted.

"I told you that. What else did the smart ass told you?" Sam barked.

"He told me something that I will pass on to my kids and they will pass it on to theirs."

"What can be that important?" Sam sneered.

"Yes, please enlighten me," Andy chuckled.

"You told me that knowledge is the true liberator."

"I believe in it," Andy smiled and remembered the walk. He was glad Ray didn't forget, and when he looked up he saw Sam was staring at him. They were eye to eye for a while then Sam turned to Ray and said with a sour throat.

"Get me one of those."

"I'll get it," Eric said and rushed to the bar.

"What knowledge can give you that basketball can't?" Sam asked, with a cough.

"Dad, knowledge gives me a freedom, you never had," Ray watched Eric coming back with the beer and after he hand it to Sam, he disappeared in his chair.

Sam stared at his son, knowing that he always wanted him to be honest, but back than he didn't know that honesty can hurt, so opening his can Sam looked away. "Raymond, you have no idea what I went through. Believe me discrimination is not easy to put up with," Sam said taking a slug from the can, and then with a faint smile he faced his son. "There were times when I would have exploded, if the training and the games wouldn't have drained my energy."

"Dad, I know our history," Ray said, staring at his father. "You're afraid that I will go through what you have, but I'm sorry I have no time for it. I am going to be a father and I have to prepare myself to guide my own kids."

"Son, there are people out there who really hates us, and if you don't know how to face them they can harm you."

"I have no problem with that."

"You don't have a problem with bigotry?"

"No. I don't have a problem with bigotry, the bigots have the problem."

"I know that," Sam shrugged.

"Dead, do you know what slavery really was?" Raymond asked, staring at his father.

"I told you we came from slaves and I don't think we should talk about it."

"No Dad, you don't know it, you feel it. Do any of you know what slavery really was?" Ray asked, looking around and Eric nodded.

"Do I know what slavery was?" Eric stated. "We English were the ones who picked them up in Africa and ship them all over the world, with the blessings of Lloyds of London."

"Can you tell me the similarities between a slave ship and an oil tanker?" Raymond asked.

"One is oil and the other one is human cargo," Eric smiled.

Andy was waiting for an answer but Sam was disturbed by the indignities of slavery. "Come on son, can we just forget about it."

"Dad, does it really hurt that much?"

"You must remember that I'm your father, and I still can kick your ass."

"Dad, we are doing it to our self, and only knowledge can liberate us from it."

"Son, I'm talking about bigotry and not algebra."

"Dad, can't you see the way intelligent people get along no matter who they are?"

"Okay, so what's your point?"

"Intelligent people are free because they constantly learning and changing with the times, the misguided think they know everything and get left behind."

"And knowledge is the true liberator," Andy said to Eric.

"What does it has to do with oil tankers and slave ships?" Sam asked.

"Their cargo was always energy." Raymond declared.

Andy was pleased with Ray's punch line and enjoyed watching Eric and Sam, as they stared at Ray with question marks in their eyes.

"Slaves were the energy and the engine around the world in every society, from the beginning of time," Ray looked around and casually continued. "Only knowledge and technology made slavery obsolete, not ethics, religion or goodwill."

"Then why did we have a Civil War?" Sam inquired.

"The slave holders limited their intelligence to suit their addictive lifestyles," Raymond continued. "They considered their way of life was God given, and when the system became obsolete they refused to part with it."

Andy nodded. "After the Civil War the freed slaves find themselves out on the streets without any rights or survival skills, and they had to start from the bottom of the social scale."

"But how a God-fearing person can do that to another human being?" Sam asked.

"The whites treated their slaves like they would their livestock, and believed that God give them the right to do with them whatever they please," Ray explained.

"You said something," Eric stressed. "I've been in many countries and there are the outcasts in every society. I noticed that people don't mind carrying their burdens as long as they can look down at someone. It's like taking a feel good placebo."

Andy nodded. It was hard for him to believe the English bum is actually a nice guy, and added. "The Indian cast system created the untouchables, for that very reason."

Sam was indignant. "Only a miserable bunch could do that to another human being."

Andy added. "Insecurity and falls pride, my friend. Insecurity and falls pride."

"Do you know that insecurity is a primitive trait?" Ray stated.

"I thought it came with our modern times?" Andy said.

"No. Insecurity is the preservation of the past and the fear of the future." Ray declared. "If it's combined with greed and incompetence, it can destroy every civilization on earth,"

"We had a retired army sergeant who was teaching us to combat fear by using our killer instincts," Sam laughed.

"Do we need our primitive killer instincts to live in a civilized society?" Eric asked.

"Good question," Andy agreed. "We don't hunt or gather anymore and we don't carry a gun to go to a supermarket, unless we want their money and not the merchandise."

"You Americans have too many guns, and guns create a violent society." Eric declared.

"Why are you Europeans so allergic to guns, don't you want to protect your property and the millions you made here in the good old U.S. of A?" Andy inquired.

"If I have a burglary I call the police. I don't want an unarmed thief to find a gun."

"Thief's usually stake out the place and enter when no one's home," Sam stated.

"But why do you have so much crime?" Eric probed.

"We are a rich country and money is the source of all evil," Sam declared.

"Do you know what money is?" Eric asked then continued. "My Hungarian drummer told me that money is the surviving tool of the reasoning beasts, in the jungle they've created."

"I have to agree, we do love money," Andy laughed.

"We like to provide our families, some people just overdo it," Sam declared.

Andy nodded. "I know some ignorant despots, who really know how to overdo it."

"Greed and intolerance old chap, it's all over the world," Eric quipped.

Andy agreed. "You're so right, and only a spiritual awakening can save us."

"Uncle Andy, you think that a prayer will help?"

"I know you don't believe in it because you're not a spiritual person, but I am."

"Don't say he's not spiritual, I know he is because he's my son."

"How can he be a spiritual if he doesn't believe in God?"

"That's his business."

"You don't have to be religious to be spiritual," Ray asserted.

"Don't you think we are one with God?" Sam asked.

"No Dad, we are one with the universe."

"What about our free spirit?" Andy asked.

"If the spirit is free, than only our misguided believes can enslave it."

"You don't have faith in God?" Sam asked, staring at his son.

"No Dad. I would like to have faith in the human race but we are not there yet."

"I know life is too complicated," Andy said.

"Of course it is," Ray said. "Life is a mental trip with a spiritual experience, and it's the most complicated think in the universe."

"You think life is more complicated than the universe?" Andy smirked.

"The universe has no secrets; it works without miracles or magic. Life is the undefined mystery because we experience it and don't know what it is," Ray defined.

"So, you think we're here once and that's it?" Sam asked.

"No Dad. The fact that we are here is the proof that we are an integral part of all this everlasting actuality, and we cannot escape it."

"Than what happens when we die?" Sam inquired.

"We will be recycled," Ray grinned.

"That's the body, what about the spirit?" Andy asked.

"If the spirit represents the individual then your presence proves that you existed at least once," Ray smiled. "If the spirit exist then chances are we will happen again, and again."

"You mean being reincarnated?" Eric asked.

Ray shrugged. "Something likes that."

"I would hate to born into the mass I have created," Eric snickered.

"Or born into a family you hated," Andy reaffirmed.

"And it can go on and on as long as earth can support us," Ray added.

"What will happen after that?" Sam asked.

"Dad, every part of our body was once inside a giant sun that exploded into a supernova, and before that we were part of the Big Bang or a Big Burst, it doesn't matter witch one. And then the elements in our body traveled through infinite space time to get to earth, and here we are."

"And you don't see God's hand in it?" Andy asked.

"No, just look around and realize that evolution is a creative process," Ray affirmed.

"If God didn't create us than why are we here?" Sam asked.

Raymond collected his thoughts and said. "To observe and verify the existence of the universe."

"It makes sense but it doesn't explain life, and even if what you said was true the source of life must be God, otherwise existence would not be spiritual," Andy declared.

"Uncle Andy, you should look at some of the pictures taken by the Hubble Telescope. They are just as awesome as the Paintings by Michelangelo on the ceilings of the Sistine Chapel, and just as much as spiritual."

"You see?" Sam turned to Andy. "You're the one who talked him into all this."

"But at least you know I never wanted him to become an atheist."

"But why are you so religious, you're worse than my wife?" Sam asked.

"I do believe in an afterlife where I can be with Dorothy, that's all."

"I know you loved her."

"And I miss her very much. The true reason I sold the house because I felt her presence."

"You mean she's in there?" Eric said with wide eyed interest.

"My wife and I spent many delightful times in the house you trying to destroy."

Eric was adamant. "You said she's back,"

"I never said that."

"You just said you felt her presence," Eric insisted.

"No not like that. In the large room with the curved windows we used to have pillows around the ledge, and every time I walk in there I can see her having tea with her friends."

"The ledge was for pillows?"

"Yes."

"You see it took up space and I removed them."

Andy just stared at Eric for a moment and not knowing what to think he continued. "When I inherited the house I was showing it to Dorothy, and up in the attic she found my great grandfather's sword from the Civil War. The sun was shining through the attic window and when she pulled out the sword and hold it up, she looked like a shining angel. I will always remember that."

"That's spooky," Eric declared.

"Why it would be spooky?" Andy inquired.

"The noise in the kitchen, I bet it was her."

"What are you talking about?"

"Now I know why you sold the place so cheap, it's hunted."

"No it's not."

"I can hardly wait to go home and tell my wife," Eric said heading to the door.

"Just hold it there you're talking about my wife," Andy exclaimed.

"Yes, walking around my house with a sword in her hand," Eric said, rushing out.

"I hate that guy," Andy said, staring after him.

"I do like his music," Ray professed.

"Why?" Andy asked when Eric returned and was holding the door open for Dolores.

She walked in waving her hands to clear the air. "What kind of place is this? Oh, there you are," She said to Ray. "She's gone into labor," Dolores said, and then she walked out.

"What?" Ray said, jumping from his chair and fallowed his mother out the door, and Eric followed him trying to keep up with Ray's strides.

Andy and Sam looked after them and they both heard Eric's excited words, "Now don't be so nervous, I want you to calm down."

The two old friends smiled at each other and Andy asked. "How tall is your wife?"

"Didi, she's about five eight or five nine, why?"

"And her son is six foot nine inch tall," Andy said, placing his hand on the top of his head, to show his height and they both said simultaneously.

"The kid's going to be a basketball player."

They finished it with a high five, and then Andy held the door open for Sam. "After you Grandpa" Then he added with a sly smile. "Or should I say, Coach?"

Outside, Sam waited for Andy to close the door then placing their arms on each other's shoulders the collaborators headed to the main house, plotting the baby's future.

CHAPTER 24

Sam measured the baby's length every day, and as time went by he regularly updated Andy about the kid's progress. When finally the kid's eyes cleared it almost gave them a heart attack. The kid didn't inherit Raymond's fierce black eyes but his mother's hazel ones, and they deliberated it in detail. They finally concluded the eyes don't matter, only the talent counts.

"It's still bad luck, having a boy with girl's eyes," Andy mumbled. "How he's going develop court awareness, or face his opponents with hazel eyes."

Andy was perplexed, shook his head and inhaled when Cilla went by and rubbed herself to his legs. Sitting on the floor she looked up at him, and Andy noticed the hair on her stomach was fully grown, and her left eye was almost as large as the right one. Cilla looked great and Andy couldn't help but notice her intrinsic femininity, many women wished they had.

Andy lifted his mug and finished his tea, and then went in the kitchen and washed it, with all the other dirty dishes in the sink. His mother told him when he was young and she visited his bachelor pad, to wash the dirty dishes before he leave the house. Andy was drying his hands when Cilla came in and jumped up on the back of a chair.

"How's my beautiful kitty?" Andy asked rubbing noses with the cat, stroking her and Cilla affectionately pressed her head against the palm of his hand, closing her eyes with trust.

Andy opened a can of savory salmon feast and held it close to the cat's nose to smell it, then pushed half the food on her tray. Mixing in the amino acid and her medicine, Andy talked to her. "Looks like you slept well last night, did you dream of catching a mouse?" Then Andy remembered, Cilla have never seen a mouse. He let her lick the spoon then placed the tray on the ground saying, "come and get it."

Andy made sure the cat have enough food and water, and went to change into his workout outfit. Going out the door Andy glanced back, and saw the cat's happily moving tail.

It was amiable to drive by the Griffith Park zoo and thinking of the animals roaming the wild, and not being kept in a full-service zoo hotel. Andy never had a chance to be around animals, his father was allergic to cats, his mother was afraid of dogs and Andy never even had a pet rock. Now driving by the zoo Andy wasn't sure that Cilla was his.

On the LA Zoo's south parking lot Andy pulled into his usual slot, and when he locked the doors he looked over his car and saw a shiny gold Porsche parked by the fence. The car looked so unique Andy pulled the hood over his head and went to check it out. The plush interior with the light green leather seats indicated a special a special order, and Andy was impressed. He checked his watch and thought that with eighteen minutes a mile, he will be done by eleven AM.

Going around the fence with a gate leading nowhere, Andy begin to count his steps. He didn't want to think about Raymond, but he quoted from an obscure concept and it bothered Andy. Raymond was about fifteen years old when he wanted to inspire Ray, and introduced him to the concept. The more Andy thought about it the guiltier he felt, and was sure the ideas in the concept influenced Raymond's young mind, and made him choose science over basketball. And it was the obscure crap that turned Raymond into a damned atheist.

Andy shuddered with remorse. He was the one who robbed the basketball world from a gifted talent, by filling his head with the goddamned ideas.

"But was the concept really that influential?" Andy wondered and started to quote from the concept: When I was growing up the stars in the night sky could mesmerize me, and in my dreams I was among them walking on the Milky Way."

Andy slowed down to let a coyote cross the road, and when he continued he saw another laying on the ground on the other side of the fence,. He stopped and they stared at each other for a few seconds, and then the intelligent beast closed her eyes, giving Andy the right of way. The communication with the coyote surprised him and he glanced back and he saw the wild beast calmly crawl from under the fence, and casually fallowed her partner. The experience lifted Andy's spirit and he placed more vigor into his steps, as he continued to recall the obscure words: "Trudging through time we made up many theories, myths and fables about the universe and our place in it but in the absence of facts most of them are just the figments of our far-fetched imaginations. There are only a few ideas worth mentioning, and one of them suggests the reason for intelligent life to evolve is to observe and verify the existence of the universe."

Andy stopped for a second because the words made sense. Andy thought that God and the Cosmos is a common identity, and the concept is not far from the truth. The only reason Andy didn't care for the obscure concept because of the many kinks in it, and he is already believed in one with just as many twists.

"There are many believe but only one truth," Andy continued when an unbelievable female figure went by, running like a pro. The incredible body slowdown and turned, and it was Domino.

She smiled and waited for Andy to catch up, "I thought it was you."

"What a pleasant surprise." Andy beamed.

"How come I've never seen you out here?" Domino asked.

"I'm here almost every morning." Andy answered.

"Ah, I run in the afternoons."

"Than what can I thank my good luck to?"

"Believe it or not this is my first free day and I'm having an early start."

"Are you done with your studies?"

"Yes. I earned my masters but now I must place it into use and this is a great place to think about it. Well, it was nice seeing you," Domino said, and continued her run.

"It was my pleasure," Andy said, and noticed how the park was not the same without her. Domino's physical assets and her running style clearly indicated she was not a stranger to track and field, and her intelligence reminded him of his good friend, her father.

"It's funny how people inherit certain traits," Andy thought.

Working with Domino's father Andy knew about his devotion to some of the woman around the Universal lot, and he never lied about them. Murphy knew how to avoid answering questions, and Andy believed that Monty was an honest man. He wasn't sure about his daughter, and believed that Domino was lying about her celibacy. "And even if it was true, with a body like hers, would be a waste."

To escape his infatuation with Domino, Andy recalled his love for Dorothy and acknowledged the way they saw the world individually. They respectfully allowed each other the freedom to express the way they felt about things, and what they liked. Andy for instance loved the sight of a beautiful woman, and he was sure that Dorothy enjoyed the sight of a good looking man. But they also enjoyed beautiful paintings, smelled the flowers or listen to pleasant sounds, without ever owning or touching any of them.

"Beauty should be respected and behold because it's so frail," Dottie used to say and her smiling face appeared affront of him.

Andy stopped to hold on to the railing by the road, and good thing he did because a few hundred students from the neighboring school were coming by in their green uniforms, and he knew that even the slowest among them was faster than he was.

Andy inhaled and watched the front bunch in step projected determent power. There was a gap for those who tried to keep up, followed by a few hundred bunched together and thinning with the stragglers.

Looking after them Andy recalled his own youthful memories and being in the tail end of his own adventures, he was wondering about their future and wished them well.

The young faces elevated Andy's spirit and decided to rejuvenate his old memories with a visit to his old neighborhood, in Atwater Village. The rest of his time in the park went fast and when he got back to the parking lot, the gold Porsche was gone.

Driving from the LA Zoo's south parking lot Andy made a left turn, and drove on Chrystal Spring Drive all the way to Los Feliz Boulevard. At the light he made a left turn and drove over Interstate five. When he reached the new shopping center Andy drove into their parking lot, and found a parking space next to a Gold Porsche.

After he locked his car Andy looked through the window of the Porsche, and recognized the green leather seats. Shaking his head in disbelieve Andy headed to the Starbucks with the long outside terrace, and in mid stride he changed his mind. He decided to visit an old friend across the street, and at the crosswalk Andy looked for the structure. When he recognized it Andy waited for the light to turn green, and with his long strides crossed the street. He walked to the building that used to be the Great Scott restaurant, with walls filled with quotations from Lord Byron, and the bar where you can order a yard of ale.

Andy went around the corner and his eyes shined at the sight of a small, white statue of a British Lyon, lying by the entrance. Andy walked up to it and wiped the bottom of his shoes on the statue's back, then kicked it gently in the butt.

With a satisfied smile, Andy calmly walked back to the crosswalk and waited for the light to change, thinking of the English bum. When Andy looked up he saw a woman was waving at him from the Starbucks' terrace, and when he lifted his hand to shade his eyes, he recognized Domino. Andy waved back and when the light turned green he floated across Los Feliz Boulevard, and up the steps to Domino. "How lucky can I get seeing you twice in the same day?" Andy smiled ear to ear.

"What were you doing across the street?" Domino asked.

"I paid tribute to an old friend." Andy smiled.

"I see," Domino said, with her sideway stare

"Can I get you anything?"

"I'm fine, thank you," Domino said sipping her coffee, watching him walk away.

Inside the coffee shop, Andy picked up the LA Times and waited in line for his turn. After he ordered his coffee, they scanned his newspaper and Andy paid. With the newspaper under his armpit and with the coffee cup in hand Andy went back to Domino's table, and took a chair. Andy thrown the newspaper on an empty chair, and sipping his coffee he looked around. "This is my old neighborhood, I used to live nearby."

"Now I live nearby," Domino clamed.

"How do you like it?"

"Love it, very cosmopolitan," Domino confirmed. "I see you still have the cat."

"Yeah, I still have it," Andy said, removing his healing hands from the table.

"Have you named it yet?"

"Yes, her name is Cilla."

"Cilla?"

"Yes Cilla, like Pris-cilla."

"Ah, Cilla," Domino mused. "Are you going to keep it?"

"I don't know. The place looks good with her in the window."

"You like her."

"She is very lady like; I mean she has that thing about her."

"You do like her."

"Well, I don't know. I mean yes, I do," Andy nodded.

They stared at each other and Andy nodded again.

"Yeah, I do love the damned cat, okay?" Andy said looking away from her and noticing an old man sitting by himself at the next table. Andy had to take another glance because the old guy was so familiar.

Andy turned to Domino and whispered. "The old guy at the next table, I think I know him just can't remember from where?"

"I saw him here yesterday," Domino whispered.

A pair of young police officers came out of Starbucks with coffee cups in their hands, and stopped a short distance away. The old man waved to them and spoke with a heavy accent.

"Excuse me, gentlemen!"

The cops looked at each other and approached the old man, positioning themselves strategically on both side of the table, blocking the escape.

"Yes Sir, what can we do for you?" The older officer asked.

"A lot of hoodlums hang around this place, disturbing people. I wonder if more police presence would scare them away."

"What do you suggest?" The older policeman asked.

"If Starbucks would give free coffee to the police, more of you would show up."

"Don't you like young man?" The younger cop asked the old man, imitating a male whore.

"I like young people, some of them are very bright," the old man stated.

"You think they are smart?" The older cop asked with a smirk, taking a step closer.

"Yes they are. But I'm not talking about them; I'm trying to tell you about the hoodlums, hanging around here,"

"I've saw you here yesterday, you do like this place don't you?" The older cop asked the Old Man with forced kindness.

"Yes, it's nice and breezy out here."

"You said we should come around more often, why don't you give me your name and phone number and I will mention what you just told me to the station commander, and he might call you back," the younger cop said to the old man, with a wink to his partner. The old man looked at the young cop and said his name, but the officer didn't understand.

"How do you spell it?"

The old man looked into the young cop's jeering face then turned to the older officer's morose one.

"Just spell it," The older cop ordered him, and the old man complied.

"What are your phone numbers?" The younger cop asked, imitating a male whore.

The old man didn't know that he was mocked and told him.

"What is your address?" The young cop asked with a tone he would like to be invited, and the older cop was staring at the Old Man like a cat would a cornered mouse.

"Just hold it there," Andy said, standing up.

Hearing the old man's accent, Andy remembered who he was and told it to Domino. They been watching what was going on and finally Andy went to the old man's side and told him. "Professor, don't say another word."

"Do you know this man?" The older cop asked, if his hands would have been cut in the cookie jar.

"Yes Sir," Andy said staring down at the cops. "He is a retired college professor of the law, and could teach you a thing or two."

"Sir, we didn't know," The young cop said, and the older officer glared at his partner.

"He's more than eighty years old, what do you think he was doing here?" Andy asked with a scolding tone, when a young couple rushed up the steps and the woman pushed herself through between the cops, and went to the old man's side.

"Grandpa, what's going on here?"

"He was telling us something, that's all," the older cop said, while the young cop lost the smirk from his face and stopped acting like a male whore.

The young man went to the old man's side, helping him from his chair. "Let's go home grandpapa, the air condition is fixed."

The old man stopped and turned to Andy. "You were one of my students at La Jolla?"

"No Sir, I met you at the Universal Studio's tower lobby. You came to visit Lou Wasserman and I escorted you to the fourteenth floor."

"Yes, yes, yes, now I remember," the old man said. "It's good seeing you again. I heard Wasserman passed away, he was a good man. Well, it was nice seeing you again." The old man waved and they left, and Andy went back to Domino's table.

"It was nice of you to intervene. This is Southern California, and people should be able to sit outside without being harassed. I just can't believe what those cops thought of him?"

"It's funny," Andy chuckled. "I can never forget the seminar when the professor lectured about the power of assumption, asserted by questionable intelligence."

"Those cops were definitely over educated, beyond their capacities." Domino smirked.

"When you get a ticket just challenge it," Andy added.

"If you don't, you lost twice," Domino declared. They were silent for a while then she asked. "The professor have a heavy accent, where is he from?"

"He's a Polish Jew. Do you know that during the Second World War their survivor rate was less than ten percent?"

"Then he's a holocaust survival," Domino emphasized, watching a young man with a pregnant wife and two young kids taking the old man's table.

Andy nodded. "Yeah, the professor is a living fossil of our resent past."

"It's hard for me to believe that civilized people can torture and kill others." Domino stated. "I heard that before Hitler, Berlin was the center of knowledge."

"Very true," Andy confirmed. "But back then only one third of the world's population knew how to read and write, and many Germans were illiterate. Don't forget that less than one third of the Germans were Nazis."

"But don't forget that you only need only one third of the population to grab power," Domino stated. "I just don't understand why they hated the Jews?"

"Throughout history, the Jews were forced to live by their intellect and unwittingly they made an evolutionary step ahead of those who use their physical strength to survive. If you noticed, Jewish people get along quite well with those who do the same. Using knowledge to survive they made more money than the ones who made a living by doing manual labor, and the Jews were able to afford an opulent lifestyle. Their wealth invited envy, and the Nazis turned that envy into hate."

"The Nazis would hate people just because they are smart?"

"Not smart, intelligent. I never trusted street smart people who claimed they knew everything," Andy smirked.

"You right, the street smarts don't know if they're outgunned with knowledge," Domino giggled.

"It takes some amount of knowledge to know how dumb we are, but some people don't even have that," Andy snickered.

"Do you think ignorance is politically motivated?"

"Yes," Andy stated. "The ones in power always ruled, by manipulating the ignorant segment of the population with lies and propaganda."

"The Nazis only manipulated a segment of the population?"

"Yes and the rest fallowed. Knowledge is the opposite of ignorance, and the stupid felt threatened," Andy smirked. "When they got rid of the Jews they wiped out half the intellectuals. They gained well educated slave labor, and just intimidated the rest of the population. The Nazis only needed the ignorant segment who believed in what they preached, and know how to take orders."

"But didn't they need intelligent people to run the country?" Domino inquired.

"The Nazi mob was ready for a war, and they needed people to supply them with food and ammunition. Their ideology created a decadent and fatalistic life style that was well demonstrated in a movie, Cabaret."

"It must have been horrible to live under those conditions?" Domino shuddered.

"The ignorant will never be able to lift you up and enlighten you. They can only pull you down to their level, and in war it's so easy to do."

"I know we all evolve in a different pace," Domino stated. "I just wasn't aware of its impact."

"It's the same all over the world. The civilized prefer to have laws to protect them, and the ignorant thinks the laws are burden, forcing them to behave like human beings."

"You think the ignorant is a lesser human being?" Domino chuckled with surprise.

"Yes, and believe me their fertile imagination can turn any paradise into hell."

"How could you say such things about another human being?"

"Because our imagination constantly works, and what we think is based on what we know. You have no idea the kind of damage a selfish and ignorant person can do."

"But one person can't know everything, we already specializing," Domino exclaimed.

"Very true, but every specialty is built on our ambient awareness."

"It would be nice to have a magic wand, and just spread knowledge around."

"Yeah, Andy moaned. "But there are no miracles or magic."

Domino was surprised. "I didn't know you were an atheist?"

Andy burst with vitriol. "How dare you call me an atheist, I'm a God-faring man."

"Excuse me. You said something I do believe in and I consider myself an atheist."

"I do love science and I'm logical, but I definitely didn't forfeit my God for it."

"I know exactly how you feel."

"How could you, you said you're an atheist?"

"I was born into a religion, just like you."

"Then what happened?"

"I just couldn't believe in an ancient story, written by people who didn't know where the sun goes at night," Domino scoffed.

"Yes, they were ignorant by today's standards," Andy stated with an understanding nod.

"You just said that ignorant people can't be trusted."

"Well, that's obvious."

"Could it be that thousands of years ago the ignorant was misguided by those who believed in miracles and magic?"

"Like Jesus defied the laws of physics, and walked on water?" Andy smirked.

"What about our parents," Domino asked. "Are they guilty for teaching us the only things they knew?"

"When we grow up, we should correct our parent's mistakes," Andy smirked.

"What if they choose a school, teaching us what they believed in?"

"It's not easy to escape our parents' influence, but sooner or later we must found out who we are and get on with our own life. I've done it."

"I'm also guilty of doing it, I'm just not sure if I benefited by it."

"If it doesn't kill you it will make you stronger," Andy lifted his fist.

"Yes, but if you do things out of sequence, you do pay for it."

"I don't think it's possible to go through life without making a mistake."

"I know," Domino nodded. "But how can we stop hurting each other?"

"I don't think we can stop loving or hurting each other on a personal level. But in any other case we have civilized options, and one of them will lead us to a common understanding."

"And what that will be?" Domino asked.

"I do believe that knowledge will be our liberator."

"Yes but don't you think that ignorance is a choice?"

"In an information age it's impossible to stop the spread of knowledge. Of course we do need a free and open mind, and we need more professors."

"I just can't get him out of my mind." Domino mused.

"Yeah, the old guy survived the Nazis, and then he came here and learned a new language."

"I heard the young couple called him grandpa, and that means a happy ending."

Domino's statement made Andy laugh. "Yes, he's still alive."

Domino was amazed. "Such a small world, he knew Wasserman?"

"Lawyers fascinated Wasserman, and I'm sure he donated to the holocaust survivors."

"When dad talked about Wasserman, he called him Lou Baby with respect. It surprised me because the only person he really liked is the one who looked back at him from the mirror."

"Wasserman deserved respect, we considered him the last mogul."

"You right, after him all the studios were swallowed up by the major corporations."

"And now they are just company assets."

"The end of an era, and I forgot to ask father about Wasserman's huge office with the ornate doors and the plush carpeting."

"Wrong." Andy snickered.

"Have I said something funny?" Domino asked.

"Wasserman's office was less than twenty by twenty feet. It was located on the fourteenth floor of the black tower's north east corner. Two of the walls were glass windows and I think the other two were just bare walls," Andy explained.

"It must have been crowded."

"No, his desk was always clean and besides his own chair, there was only another one affront of his desk. The only outstanding object in the room was George Washington's iron cane, standing near his desk in a tall, pyramid shaped Plexiglas case."

"I heard it was Wasserman's statement," Domino concurred.

"Yes, but if you knew him he was down to earth. He was in touch with every aspects of the industry, and he personally inspected everything. Wasserman knew almost everybody on the Universal lot."

"Did he ever get mad?"

"No. Wasserman was always in control," Andy said. "He used his power to direct, and he never abused it."

Domino differed. "I heard it differently,"

"He had a strong presence and that could have been misunderstood." Andy stated. "Being tall, slim and with those glasses, I'm sure he knew who he was."

"You right, dad talked about his aura."

"Wasserman was also a visionary; he personally inspected and approved the design of every new building on the lot."

"Dad told us when Wasserman choose the oil green color for the Texaco Building."

"I was there," Andy reminisced. "And the construction was almost done, when the Santa Anna winds blew all the windows out, and the Hollywood Freeway had to be shut down to save people from the flying glass."

"Oh yes, I saw it on the news," Domino said. "And I thought they only made movies."

Every studio is like a city," Andy stated. "They have a Security Department and a Fire House with real fire man. They have electricians, plumbers, locksmiths, carpenters, painters and a host of other trades. And Wasserman was the major and the master of ceremonies."

"He's the boss, Dad used to say."

"Yes he was."

"It's hard to believe that with all his power he was so approachable."

"He had his morning coffee in the Commissary, right at the counter."

"It sounds almost disappointing," Domino giggled.

"Let me tell you something I was personally involved. On the fifteenth floor of the black tower was the original office of Jules Stein, the founder of MCA. From the fourteenth floor a wide staircase, and also a small elevator went up to it. The fifteenth floor had a kitchen just outside the office door, and next to it was the theater. Under the projector's window was a white feather couch, where Jules Stein used to watch the just finished movies. A full screen was pulled out from the wall, and covered the windows to darken the room. The theater was also a conference room, and after Jules Stein passed away Wasserman wanted to update the place. He made me charge of the project, and I sent out an order to the Electric Department for the installation of three rows of lights on the ceiling, above the conference table. They sent out John and Craig, two good men who earlier installed the pole lights outside the black tower. I wanted five lights in each row that can be turned on and off, and also dimmed. When the job was done Wasserman, Dorskin and Sheinberg came up to inspect it, and I found them playing with the switches like kids."

Domino was surprised. "The most powerful people in Hollywood played like kids?"

"Yes. The creators and the masters of the Universal octopus, played like children."

"No wonder their team parks pulls people from all over the world, and bedazzle them."

"Are you talking about the tour center up on the hill?" Andy inquired.

"Yes, and the one in Florida and the one in Japan."

"I didn't even think about them," Andy chuckled.

"What do you think drove Wasserman?"

"It had to be his devotion to Jules Stein, proving to him the company was in good hands."

"I met Wasserman, and I can never forget the way his smile light up the place."

"Yes he could be very charming, but he kept his eyes on everything. I told you about the conference room on the fifteenth floor. Wasserman hold meetings in there with the managers of the Amphitheater, the tour centers, the heads of music, film and other interests. Each individual was a powerful man in their own domain, but if anything ever happened to one of Wasserman's babies, they get a tong lashing they never forget. I saw many of them run out of the room to throw up in that ridiculously claustrophobic toilet, with a stupid chandelier."

"That's what I was referring to when I asked if Wasserman ever got mad. I just never knew the Black Tower had a toilet with a chandelier?" Domino giggled.

"Yes they do," Andy nodded.

"You must have had a wonderful life?" Domino mused.

"And I'm thankful. What about you, have you figured out what are you're going to do?"

"Well, starting out on something new and being a woman I do have some advantages, but all for the wrong reasons," Domino shrugged. "Otherwise if you're not sure of yourself it could be very lonely, and being a sex object it doesn't help."

"Come on, it can't be that bad," Andy smiled with encouragement.

"You want a bet?" Domino sneered, and the smile left Andy's face.

"You should go out with your boyfriend and have a few drinks."

"I told you I was celibate."

"You could have fallen off the wagon," Andy said, but couldn't hold a straight face, and staring at each other they snickered. "So what have your celibacy done for you lately?"

Domino inhaled through her nose, and gestured with her hands. "It gave me an unbelievable freedom, and mental strength."

"You're kidding me."

"Celibacy helped me realize that I was guided by my animal instincts, and not by my human reasoning."

"I know exactly what you mean."

"Do you really?"

"Well, I'm not you but yes, very much so," Andy nodded.

"Then you do know when you're celibate, you see life through a one way mirror."

"No not that one," Andy said enthusiastically.

"In our world sex is the most important commodity, and when you refuse to participate it's like watching life through a one way mirror. And no one knows you are on the other side."

"Yes, life does become more valuable when you have control over your primitive urges."

"Exactly, and believe me, nobody ever died from the lack of sex," Domino stated, and watched Andy swallow and look away.

Sipping her coffee, Domino gently bit her lip as she examined Andy. It was a long time ago at lunch time when she followed him and her father to the Le Petit Chateau, on Lankershim Boulevard, and found out that Andy was one of her father's closest friends. Now that she was talking to him she found him interesting.

"You're so right," Andy said, staring at Domino's mouth, and her breasts. "We are at a point in life when we should consciously think of ourselves as humans, guided by our intellect and not by our primitive urges."

Andy tasted his coffee and then he turned to spit it out, but seeing the kids at the next table he grimaced and swallowed it. "This coffee tastes horrible."

"Do you want some of mine?" Domino asked and poured her coffee into Andy's cup.

"No, have some of mine," Andy said and poured the coffee back into her cup.

The young man with the pregnant wife and the two kids was watching them pour coffee into each other's cups. The woman looked like a movie star and the guy had to be at least ten years older than she was. He dealt with his type before through his construction business, and found most of them clumsy, selfish and stupid. He proudly looked at his beautiful kids and his pregnant wife and sent a mental massage to the rich guy. "You may have a best looking girl in town boy, but you don't have a family like mine."

Watching the couple, he noticed they stopped pouring coffee into each other's cup and saw her dip her index finger into her coffee than placed it into her mouth. Staring at each other the numbed nuts finally got the massage and dipped his index finger into his coffee, and placed his thumb in his mouth. The woman put her tennis shoes on top of his and the guy instantly moved his leg away, placing his hand firmly on the table.

"Why would he do that, is he married?" The young man mused, and watched her placing her hand on top of his, stroking it. She whispered something and the guy placed his foot back on the table's leg, and the woman eagerly placed her foot on top of his.

They stroked each other's hands than holding it they stood up and made a few steps, and then he placed his arm around her shoulders and she placed hers around his waist. The young family man was surprised to see them acting like kids, stepping affront of each other and then she bumped him with a laugh and run away. The rich guy run after her, and the young family man noticed the newspaper they left behind. He rushed over and held the newspaper up waving it after them, and then slowly acknowledged that they will not be interested in the news for a while.

CHAPTER 25

It was a worm evening with the sun hanging on the horizon, and the parking lot was still full of cars. The parking lot guard was standing in her favorite spot, where she was able to watch the place and only a few people would glance in her direction and notice her impressive presence.

Jazz was a big woman, barefoot she was over six foot two with large breasts and large buts. She was holding a flashlight, big enough to stop a charging bull. Jazz also carried a stunt gun, a pepper spray and a phone to call the police in case she needed them. Jazz was an intimidating figure but today she was wearing Betsy's presents, a pair of comfy shoes. Thinking of her she thankfully wiggled her toes, as she contently glanced around her domain.

People have no idea what a good pair of shoes can do to folks working on their feet, it placed a smile on her face and Jazz would never do that intentionally. She liked her job and tried to be calm and in control, without showing any emotion.

Actually Jazz liked to smile but only at the ones she loved, but there were not many of them. Her father wanted a boy and from the very beginning he hated her and named her Jezebel, but her mother loved her and she called her Jazz. She found out early in life that being a black woman with a father like hers is like hitting the wall right after she was born.

Jazz didn't want to be timid like her mother, but being underage and insecure she had no other choice but to accept the conditions. But it was not easy, her father was verbally abusive and the only reason Jazz and her mother put up with it because they knew the source of his frustration. He wanted to be a good but it was hard for a black man to curve out a decent living in a bigoted society. Jazz's father was in constant despair, and one day she found him in their bedroom slipping in a heroin haze. He was rude but not brutal like her girlfriend's father was across the street. That man was always drunk, and called his wife and daughter whores. Jazz saw them running away when he tried to bit them up.

Jazz knew that her father was a miserable creature and he only had his anguish to spread around, but she was hoping for better days. But her father's drug addiction got worse, and when her mother inherited the house, she also received thirty thousand dollars in cash. Jazz thought the money will help them out but her father found out about it, and he wanted it. They gave it to him under one condition, that he lives the house and never come back. Exactly one month later they found his dead body in a chip hotel room with a needle in his arm, and not enough money in his pockets for the funeral.

Jazz and her mother cleaned people's homes for a living. Working and going to school she was always busy, and Jazz turned fourteen without ever having a boyfriend. She was working for a rich couple when the lady of the house noticed her young, developing body and asked her to make some lemonade and take it down to the pool.

When Jazz arrived the lady of the house was but naked in the pool, and invited Jazz to join her. When she toke off her close and got close to her, the woman touched her breasts and she enjoyed it. Back than Jazz didn't know that she was taken advantage of, and their offer lasted almost a year. During that time she never thought of herself as a lesbian, because Jazz believed in marriage she just didn't know with whom.

When Jazz turned fifteen, she fall in love with a football player and their first time together was in the back seat of his car, on a hill, overlooking the school's football stadium. He just had to touch her and Jazz was in ecstasy, and her love of him made her easy to please. Those were the happiest times of her life, and it hurt that much more when Jazz saw him walking on the campus with his arms around another girl.

Loving him so much she couldn't blame him, so Jazz hated the girl like she never hated anyone before, and was ready to kill the bitch. She went through a lot of mental anguish, and finally Jazz confessed to her minister. The priest helped her realize the girl she hated was just another victim of the school structure, favoring their football team. It was the time when they thought her in school that everybody's born equal but wherever she went people talked down to her, even though she was a lot taller than most.

"Being black and woman, is like a curse with the double whammy," Jazz smirked, and looked around if anyone see her doing it.

The young man from the soup kitchen came out for his usual cigarette brake and leaned back, with one foot against the wall. Jazz talked to him a few times and found out that he was thirty-two years old, a year younger then she was. The man was married with kids, and already had the same sad smile on his face, her father had.

He told her about growing up in a gang, and the difficulties he faced when he left them. Jazz knew that gangsters were heavy on drugs, and it made her question his mental health. She dated a gang member and knew they were just a ruthless bunch, living off of the already suffering population. Jazz found them ignorant, and just to show how mucho they are they abuse their women. When the very first time her boyfriend hit her, Jazz grabbed his arm and broke it. Before Jazz left, she gave him a black eye and the gang let her walk away. None of the members liked women, having their own minds. To regain some of his dignity her ex-boyfriend went after her, and Jazz broke his other arm. She heard it that he lost rankings in the gang, and his name was changed from Spider to Stinky.

Being an adult Jazz enjoyed sex and dated, but most man turned out to be unsatisfactory one night stands, and not one of them cared how she felt. Many times she had to watch their ridiculous grin on their satisfied faces, as they zipped up their limp manhood. And when they left she had to finish the job.

Jazz had friends whose husbands slapped them around at least once a week, they needed or not. And every one of them talked about their husbands if they would have been their property. While the women was faithful the man was always on the prowl, and some of them infected their wives with their diseases. She heard of places where the man was so selfish and insecure, they circumcise their woman and rub them from their sexual pleasures. Jazz begin to think that men don't love women at all, and was glad she learned martial arts in school.

A car's alarm went off, and when she located the source she recognized the deaf lady who runs a small Boutique. The woman must have had an indicator inside her car, because she turned off the alarm.

The lady was classy and Jazz liked her. She can never forget the day when the lady drove by waving to her, not knowing the car's alarm was on. Jazz even felt guilty for telling her about it, by opening and closing her hands. She can never forget the lady's surprising motion of apology. It was hard for Jazz to understand how a nice person like her can live in a world of silence, without any music.

An Oriental man in his suit and necktie, erectly walked by, and ten paces behind him his wife fallowed. Only Jazz noticed them because in this neighborhood people behave the way they always do. Being on the job for over a year Jazz learned so much she can pair people with their cars, and could tell if she could trust them or not.

The neighborhood was diverse and Jazz was able to see the world's religions marching by. She was able to recognize the Sikhs and the Muslims from their turbans, and knew the difference. Jazz only had trouble with the Oriental people; she never knew who were the Chines, the Japanese, or the Korean.

On her first day on the job Jazz was so impressed seeing people from all over the world she dreamed about them at night, and her next day became a surreal experience.

She liked her job but standing on her feet all day was not easy, and the pay was terrible. If she wouldn't be living with her mother, she won't be able to pay her rent.

A horn went off and her eyes searched the lot, but it was only a guy opening his car door without turning off his alarm. Since Jazz toke over the night shift they only had one burglary, and she got the culprit. By the time Jazz handed him over to the police the poor guy was glad to be handcuffed, and the word must have gone around. Jazz remembered the incident because the boy was black, and she wondered if she would have treated him differently if he would have been someone else. Having this job she came to realize that some of the black folks feel like newcomers into the white man's world, and some of them are quite sensitive if they don't get accepted right away. She noticed the well to do blacks don't have any trouble melting in, and they do behave like they belong.

What Jazz really enjoyed was watching the school kids. They all looked so bright, and none of them show any racial prejudice. They treated each other equally and it gave Jazz hope for the future.

She also saw the hustlers, the pimps, the whores, and the thieves lurking around, looking for human weaknesses and ready to pounce. Every day Jazz begin her shift remembering the sign on her boss's desk, "When the pray is out the predators are not far behind."

Jazz tasted the good life so rarely she felt guilty when she had it. She was penniless most of her life but she never once thought about selling herself. Jazz was not a moralist but she was truly disgusted when she saw, what people are capable of doing for money. Jazz called the police on some but they were back the very next day, arrogantly smirking at her, and the male whores were worse. Now days she just knocks with her flashlight on the car's window, if they get too noisy or obvious.

Jazz shifted her weight and wiggled her toes again, every time she became negative she just thought of Betsy, and it cheered her up. It was four years ago when Jazz weight only 170 pounds, when she met this tall, handsome man with a bald head. He toke her to exotic places and after partying all night, they gone home and made love. When they woke up they made love till four or five in the afternoon, and then they got ready to party all over again. One day he just disappeared, and Jazz never saw him again.

She waited for him for two years, and went from 170, up to 306 pounds. It took her two years to go down to 250, and Jazz promised to God if she could go down to two hundred she will go church every Sunday.

Even though she has a long way to go, losing fifty six pounds lifted her self-esteem, and she credited it to Betsy. Knowing that without her she would never have made it, Jazz smiled and remembered the day they met.

Just about two years ago it was a hot summer weekend and her mother went to her churches Bingo parlor, and Jazz decided to visit Fern Dell Drive. She learned about the place watching Huell Howser's California Gold, and heard it was the coolest place in town. On some weekends the Los Angeles freeways are practically empty, and in no time Jazz was on Los Feliz Boulevard. Just before it curves south and turns into Western Avenue, Jazz turned North on Fern Dell Drive, and parked her car near the restaurant.

Jazz walked down the embankment, crossed a bridge and was on a dirt road next to a stream. The trees, the bushes, the water and the lush semi tropical landscape kept the place nice and cool. The railings and the resting spots with benches were all made of wood, and the greens and the trees gave the place a shaded ambience.

The road was curvy, slanting downward, and after Jazz went under a bridge. At a pleasant curve with a two foot waterfall, she rested on a wooden bench. Jazz leaned back closing her eyes, and stretched her arms on the back of the bench. She inhaled the fresh air, and when she opened her eyes she was able to see patches of blue sky, through the tree's canopy. Jazz closed her eyes again and listened to the waterfall, when a weird sound was getting closer, and closer. Suddenly a tiny red headed woman with a red freckled face and in a soaking wet green tracksuit appeared, and collapsed on the other end of the bench.

"Are you okay?" Jazz asked.

Catching her breath the woman nodded. "I'm sorry, I know it's non-of your business but I decided to lose weight and it turned out to be a son of a bitch," the woman said.

"Tell me about it," Jazz said with raised eyebrows. Watching the woman looking at her three hundred and six pound body.

"You're a big woman, you can handle it, I'm less than five four and it just weighs me down," the woman said, pulling up her shoulders and pocking her stomach. "I don't even know how it happened, one day I woke up and I was fat."

"Tell me about it," Jazz smirked.

The woman lifted her hand. "By the way, my name is Betsy."

"Call me Jazz," she said, and the two of them shook hands. Jazz can never forget her worm and friendly smile, and her small white hand with all those light brown freckles. And for reasons unknown and cannot be explained, she opened up and told her things she would never tell anyone. Before they parted they placed each-others phone numbers into their cellphones, and had a good laugh when they called to make sure it rings. They became good friends and found out they both had similar experiences with man, only Betsy was too small to retaliate, and the guy wasn't even a gang member. When Betsy invited Jazz to her place for diner, they finished a bottle of wine and kissed.

One night Jazz confessed and told Betsy that she hated her body, and saw Betsy as a petite red headed beauty. In turn Betsy told Jazz that she hated her freckles, and thought she was ugly. Jazz couldn't help but smile at the thought, as she glanced over the parking lot. Her eyes stopped on a black Cadillac and a gold Porsche parked next to each other. She marked their tiers because none of the employees can afford them, and they were far-far over their two our limits. Jazz became curious, and she wanted to know who they belong to.

Jazz wiggled her toes and when she looked up the soup kitchen guy was gone, and she noticed the major stores were closed. Many of the cars left and the parking lights were turned on. The moon shined brightly and Jazz saw a couple slowly stroll from Los Feliz Boulevard in to the parking lot. They stopped between the Porsche and the Cadillac, and he leaned her against the car. With his left arm around her waist the guy was kissing her, and was foundling her breasts with his right. It was getting very interesting and when his right hand went between her legs. Jazz thought they are going to make it out right there, when she heard the woman say.

"No, don't, not here."

"He wants her again," Jazz wondered, wiggling her toes. "What did they do all this time, playing dominoes?"

Jazz knew only one man who wanted her that much but he disappeared and sometimes she thought it was a dream. She came to believe that a man like that doesn't exist. She heard of knights in shining armor, but hers wasn't even in rags on a donkey.

Jazz heard a giggle and they were back kissing and touching each other, and Jazz was able to see her bare breast in the moonlight.

"Stop it," She said, buttoning her blouse.

She kissed him on the chick and after she unlocked her car he opened the Porsche's door. When she got in and started the engine, she lowered the window and he was immediately inside, with his mouth on hers and his hand on her breasts. Finally the guy pulled himself out of the car, stepped back and Jazz heard her say.

"Save it for me and I will save it for you."

The man thrown a kiss and waved after her leaning against his car, and immediately a male whore from Starbucks appeared.

"What a jerk," Jazz mumbled, lifting her flashlight and hitting the guy with its beam. She calmly watched him cover his eyes, and Jazz moved the beam in a hush away gesture. The bottom-feeding low life scum showed Jazz his middle finger, and walked away.

The man at the Cadillac never knew that he was watched, got in his car and drove away. Standing in the dark Jazz replayed in her mind what she just saw, and it aroused her. She remembered the night when Betsy admitted that she awakened in her a little girl, and now Jazz was wondering if a man like that could do the same for her.

"The reason we have fairytales," Jazz thought, looking around a now barely lighted and thinning parking. Suddenly she was engulfed by a sad and lonely feeling, with a cold she never felt before, and she didn't know if the chill was coming from inside of her. Her entire life flashed by with all its sadness and like an outcast, Jazz looked up at the moon and wanted to howler.

"Yes I'm black, and yes I'm a woman! I'm a human being, and I'm strong and I'm here, and I always bee here!"

But she was silent and inside of her a little girl cried out and was longing for Betsy's smile, her beautiful soul and Jazz wanted to kiss her every dot. A horn sounded and Jazz turned to see who it was, and then Jazz sniffed, reached into her pocket for a paper napkin, and wiping her eyes she mumbled. "Now I can't see the fucking parking lot."

CHAPTER 26

Sam Dart was the happiest man in the world. It was the wedding of his son and the baptism of his grandson: Samuel Raymond Dart the Third. Sam invited all his friends, and ordered the best food and wine money can buy, and Andy thought the sea food on ice was first rate.

Sam's euphoria infected everybody, and under its spell Dolores was able to talk Melody into her wedding dress and Raymond into his tuxedo. She was ready to have a phony wedding, with a phony priest, in her small phony chapel, and it was well photographed for posterity. They only had a small malfunction with the bride's dress. There was a wet spot where the milk comes out. But Dolores insisted on taking the pictures, and retouches them latter. Thinking of the phony wedding Andy knew Dolores was a hypocrite but with all her faults she was a good Christine.

Andy walked into the food tent and picket up a paper plate and a plastic fork. He picked the best looking giant shrimps and lobster meat, and placed two French rolls on the side. With a glass of champagne Andy headed outside to a wood bench under a tree. Andy mixed the wine with the food in his mouth, and munched it to enjoy the taste. He glanced at the fifty or so casually dressed well-known sport figures, and their families. They were in their lunge chairs, or just lay on the ground. There were kids playing and guys throwing balls and Andy was amazed to see the many friends Sam had.

Earlier Andy watched Sam talking to Magic Johnson, and now he was discussing something with Jerry West. Andy met Karrim Abdul-Jabbar and thought he was very tall, just like his Godson Raymond. He was talking to Dolores, when the Williams sisters called from Paris. "Is there anyone in sport, they don't know?" Andy wondered.

The other thing was that Andy more than six foot four tall, and wherever he was he stick out, but in this crowd he was just an average height.

Andy glanced in the direction of the house next door and even though he couldn't see it where he was, he knew it was there. Andy tried not to think of the present owner, and took a deep breath and forced the damned Limey from his mind, and was thinking of his cat. He felt sorry for Cilla being home all by herself, and wondered what she was doing. Andy felt guilty for living her alone, but this time he didn't have much choice. Now he wished that he would have had animals around the house, because with Cilla and the three adorable kittens he saw in the store, he would have never sold his house to the damned Limey. He would even have a dog, and may have let Domino move in with him.

"But what Dorothy would think?" Andy wanted to tell her about Domino, and then he came to realize that in heaven she's already know. He tried to be logical about loving two women in the same time, and wasn't sure if he should nurture his everlasting love of Dorothy, while he was satisfying his animalistic hunger with Domino.

Enjoying both women with all his senses Andy was mildly surprised when he realized, that both women opened windows to him and let him pick in and see, who they really are. Without the protection of their feminine mystic, Andy was ready to blend his soul with theirs, when he suddenly realized that both of their names started with a D.

Biting into the last shrimp, Andy wanted to throw the paper tray into the green container but it was too far, and he went over and dropped it in. Andy wandered around with his glass of champagne in hand, and noticed the net was removed from the tennis court, and had the cages setup for basketball. Andy heard someone was playing a piano, and he fallowed the sound. It was coming from the small chapel, with the six foot tall glass cross on the door. Andy couldn't see through the opaque glass, so he went to the side of the building where the melody was sipping through an open window.

Andy leaned against the wall and listened to the Chopin peace. He forgot the name of the tune, but remembered when Arthur Rubinstein was playing it on PBS. Andy was able to visualize the great man with his eyes closed, and his fingers floating over the keys, guided by his soul. Andy knew it can't be the master because he only plays to God. But then who is the genius on the piano?

Andy picked through the window and saw Dolores with her friends seating in the pews, but he couldn't see the performer who effortlessly changed from the Chopin peace to Franz Liszt's Libenstadt. Andy felt like rushing in and found out who was on the keys, but it would disturb the maestro and that would be a sacrilege. Andy didn't want the pleasant sound to end, and he leaned against the wall and closed his eyes, moving his champagne glass to the tune.

The player's fingers were so light with just the right touch, only years and years of practice can achieve, and its tenderness illustrated the person's maturity. Andy learned it from experience that only a person of wisdom and grace can play such a beautiful way, when he heard Eric's cockney voice.

"Ladies, I really like the classics but let me play my thru love," and Eric started playing Jerry Lee Lewis' Great Balls of Fire.

"Hold it, hold it," Andy heard Dolores' demanding voice. "This is a Holly place."

"Yes it is you stupid Limey bum," Andy mumbled in disillusionment, and his shaking hand almost poured the champagne on himself.

Andy inhaled deeply and stretching his neck left and right, Andy turned the corner and saw the women coming from the chapel. When Eric came out and saw Andy, he walked right up to him. "Good thing I saw you old chap, you told me you worked for the studios?"

"Yes, for Universal. Why?" Andy said.

"Then you are AD Flowers, the stunt man."

"No. AD Flowers was an Academy Award winning special effects man."

"Then who are you?"

"I'm a retired executive."

"Ah," Eric exclaimed with a disappointed tone.

"May I ask you something?" Andy asked.

"Yeah, shoot."

"Where did you learn to play the piano like that?"

"At London's City Collage."

"You learned to play like this in a city college?"

"Yes, many of our great musicians graduated from it."

"You're kidding?"

"Why should I kid you?"

"You know Eric you're wasting your talent on Rock and Roll."

"I'm wasting my talent on Rock And Roll?"

"Yes, you could be a great concert pianist. "

"I am a concert pianist."

"Then why you play primitive rock and roll?"

"Because it's primitive and tells it like it is."

"Don't you think it's below you?"

"It would be below me if I didn't."

"What do you mean by that?"

"It would be like, missing out on a day."

"That noise makes sense to you?"

"Just listen to the words and then you will understand the noise."

"Ah." Andy said, staring at Eric and feeling sorry for him.

"Music always expressed our primitive desires and it only changes with the times."

"Ah." Andy said, trying to catch up.

"It's just another form of expression of life."

"You mean like the national anthem, expressing the love of a country?" Andy asked.

"Exactly. By the way, why you guys play it at every chance you've get?"

"What do you mean every chance we get?"

"You should think about playing your national anthem on special occasions and start your baseball games without it."

"Start a baseball game without the national anthem, are you nuts?"

"It should only be played in the beginning of an international game, but not many countries play baseball, so you play your anthem every chance you have."

"Baseball is big in Japan, and even Castro played it in Cuba?"

"Yes, but you don't play many games with Cuba."

"We don't deal with dictators, or with oppressive regimes."

"Tell that to the Iranians."

"What about the Iranians?"

"Remember the Shah? You put him in power and just look what happened."

"That was a long time ago and we wanted to be fair."

"How can you be fair when you've taken sides in religious conflicts? You should learn the future is the consequence of the past."

"It's easy to be a critic after the game is over."

"All your mistakes are just games to you, no wonder you make so many of them?"

"We don't make mistakes."

"What about the war in Viet Nam?"

"We were there to stop the spread of Communism."

"But Viet Nam is now a communist country."

"Thank you, you just proved my point."

"What about Iraq?" Eric sneered.

"What about Iraq?" Andy spitting it out.

"Just by being between Iran and Saud Arabia, Sadam Hussein held the balance of power in the Middle East. He was also on the CIA payroll, and you turned on him."

"He could have had nuclear weapons."

"But he didn't."

"You know darn well we looked for it."

"Yes, and in the process you turned the country into a no-man's land."

"It was radicle Islam, not us."

"Let me just tell you something," Eric continued. "If I would make as many mistakes as you have, I would try to found out what am I doing wrong?"

"We all make mistakes it's the best way to learn, but you sure like to bitch a lot. What's wrong with you, are you missing the sun that set on your empire?"

"You are the leader of the free world, and we fallowed you into every mass you've created. Can you just keep us out of it?"

"You do have a big mouth now, you tend to forget that we saved your hide twice."

"You never let us to forget it. Now let me tell you something, I'm glad we fought our common enemy in boat wars side by side, but I never knew we had to thank you for it?"

"Without us, you would be speaking German by now."

"I don't think so, but it's always nice to know how our allies think of us."

"You the one who came here and said we are doing everything wrong."

"No not everything."

"Than what are you babbling about?"

"America is a technological force, and started the information age. The computer and the printer made the typewriter obsolete, and with the cellphone you changed the world."

"I know all that."

"You also toke the leash off the beast you've created, knowing with all its greed it will devour its masters."

"What kind of nonsense are you talking about?"

"I'm talking about your freewheeling capitalistic system. It works great when under strong democratic controls, but you removed the restrictions and its greed will destroy everything."

"I don't think you understand the free market system, we always build and only destroy to build something new in its place. And it works best without restrictions."

"If that's what you like to believe its fine with me, it's your country. But you should taste the drinking water in some of the places, and do you know your roads and bridges are falling apart. I wouldn't take a train ride anywhere in your country."

"We have the best railroad system in the world, and our roads are first rate."

"It used to be when you where the defender of Democracy, and your government controlled the beast. I remember when you used to break up monopolies and protected the environment."

"You don't know what you're talking about. Our economic system made us the richest country in the world."

"Not anymore. You're already the victim and you don't even know it."

"What the hell are you talking about?"

"You are the only country in the world where corporations are considered people. And when the corporate money buys the loyalty of your senators, and congressmen the balance of power shifts and haywires the capitalistic system."

"I heard this crap before. Don't forget we have buried communism a long time ago?"

"Wake up, your country owes over twenty trillion dollars, and the interest alone enslaved your future. When you removed your democratic controls from your corporations they stopped serving the American people, and now the beast holds the leash."

"I don't think you understand us at all."

"Don't you see where you are heading? Your economic system enslaved the American people, and one third of your population will be homeless and the other third will be in jail."

"If you don't like it here why don't you go back to your socialist shithole?"

"I'm going. I sold the house and more than doubled my money."

"Don't forget to pay your taxes and choke on the rest."

"I won't be paying much taxes, I've have a lot of deductions for the improvements I made."

"You call them improvements you dumb, limey bastard?" Andy said and was ready to pounce on the guy.

"And you're a great American asshole. Get a cape and jump off a tall building," Eric said, showing Andy his middle finger.

"What's going on here?" Sam asked, rushing up to Andy.

"It's that stupid limey jerk. If he doesn't like it here then he should go back where he came from."

Sam "He sold the house and going back to England."

"I know, he told me," Andy shrugged.

Sam took a long look at him.

"Then, what's wrong?" Sam asked, staring at Andy.

"What is he going to do with all that money in a socialist country?"

"England is not a socialist country."

"I know. It's a kingdom with a queen, but they have social medicine."

"Come on, that won't make them socialists."

"That's how it starts," Andy stated. "One day you're free, and the next day you're one of them."

"But what if he's right?"

"My God, he brainwashed you already?"

"Why would you say that?"

"You are favoring socialism over our old tried and true."

"Our old tried and true was a bigoted, racist society."

"But we came a long way," Andy said, staring at Sam.

Sam glared back, and then grinned. "We sure did brother, we sure did."

Sam placed his arm on Andy's shoulder and pushed him toward the basketball court, but Andy stopped. "Where's Raymond?"

"My wife wore them out, and I think they are resting."

"I know, the phony wedding was so unnecessary," Andy said with a timid smile.

"After the wedding Melody had it out with Dolores."

"But I thought they get along just fine?"

"Melody and Ray wanted a civil ceremony, that's all."

"So?"

"After the phony wedding in the chapel Melody told Dolores, that her religion was a self-induced mental disease."

"How could she say such things, she seems like a nice young woman."

"They are atheists."

"Ah yeah, I forgot," Andy said, and remembered the day when he gave the obscure concept to Ray, and the thought almost made him lose the seafood he just had.

"Are you okay?" Sam asked and Andy nodded.

"I'll be all right," Andy said, taking a deep breath and was thinking about making up a list of things he should never mention to Sam.

"Come on Andrew," Sam said, hanging his arm on Andy's shoulder. "Just look around its Southern California, the sun shines and there's always a breeze."

"I'm sorry," Andy said, looking around and seeing all the healthy faces.

"I almost forgot to tell you, we want you to be the referee in a basketball game," Sam said, and hung a blue string with a whistle onto Andy's neck.

"I can't, I don't have the eyes for it," Andy said, trying to take the whistle off, but Sam stopped him.

"The game is for fun, and the players will enjoy the mistakes."

"Who's going to be playing?"

"You'll see them when they come out," Sam said and left.

Holding the shiny whistle hanging from his neck, Andy blew into it and everybody stopped and stared, waiting for someone to tell them what to do.

Andy shrugged and with a stupid grin went to the basketball court, and took a chair. He looked up at Mount Wilson Observatory, and was thinking of all the famous people who visited the place and his faith was reassured when he remembered, they were all God-fearing people.

"If I'm on the right track what kind of road Ray and Melody was on?" Andy pondered when a couple appeared holding hands and their tall silhouettes almost filled the setting sun. The sight was so perfect that Andy's heart skipped a beat when he realized, it was Melody and Ray. It was like watching the future step out of the sun, and when they were recognized, the others surrounded them. Andy watched the youthful faces and was almost glad he was not one of them.

The future is unclear and the population of the world is out of control. The rising ocean waters already pushing people inland and the religious wars in the Middle East displaced millions of people. The growing population creates more trash, and with all the plastic in the seas the future is not very bright. Global warming will create catastrophic tornados, and some of the world's shorelines will become inhabitable. Wormer water will kill the fish, and all the wild animals, including cats. The microscopic plastic pieces in the air and on the surface of the water will found their way into our food supply. Without the rainforest and with the polluted sea, earth will run out of oxygen, and the end for life will soon follow.

Even if we would stop burning the Amazon forest and stop polluting right now, to clean the environment would take all the money we spend on the armies of the world an entire year, and nobody would commit themselves to that sacrifice. Andy believed that mankind long past the time when it was possible to save the world, because nobody would discard their tribal interests for the benefit of all.

"But the end will not be here for a while," Andy thought. "And he and his cat will live through the beginning of it."

Andy heard that cats can live for twenty years, and he also hoped to be here to verify it. But thinking of Cilla being home alone, it made Andy wondered what she was doing?

When Cilla was little she always waited for him by the front door, but now days she sits on the window ledge. Andy visualized Cilla in his apartment window all by herself and felt guilty for not bring her along. But he can't keep Cilla in a cage all day, and if he let her out she can get lost. Cats are not like dogs, she won't be able to find her way home if she gets lost.

Sitting on the basketball court all by himself with his dismal thoughts, Andy didn't know that he was sticking out in the happy crowd like a sore thumb. When Raymond noticed it he touched his wife's arm and left her with friends, and went to see Andy.

"Uncle Andy, what are you doing here all by yourself?" Raymond asked.

"I'm thinking about my poor cat, being home all alone."

"Don't worry, cats like to be alone."

"Not true, they are social animals with a curious individuality."

"Well, that's what I heard."

"People who never had pets should have their mouth shot."

"You do like your cat."

"Yes I do love my Cilla."

Uncle Andy, can I tell you something?"

"Shoot."

"I think you look happier since you have the cat."

"I think you right," Andy laughed. "I learned a lot from Cilla."

"You learned from a cat?" Raymond snickered.

"You be surprise how much you can learn having animals around. It's another dimension of life."

"Uncle Andy, what a wonderful idea. I think I get to my son a baby dog and a baby cat."

"Yeah, let them grow up together."

"And take a lot of pictures of them," Raymond blurted.

"Pets can expend his world, I know it enhanced mine."

"I tell you what, I look into it tomorrow," Raymond promised.

"By the way," Andy exclaimed. "After the wedding you disappeared and I never had a chance to congratulate you."

"We had some problems with Mom, and Mellow wanted to leave."

"I heard about it. Where's the baby?"

"Asleep."

"Is someone's watching?" Andy asked with concern.

"He's with his nanny."

"I do worry about his future. I been watching the news and reading the newspapers, and it's hard for me to believe what's going on."

"Good you're catching up."

"We left a mass to your generation."

"We know that."

"Is it true we are indebted, close to twenty trillion dollars?"

"I think it's more than that."

"That damned limey."

"What about the limey?"

"Ah, it's nothing. Do you know, there's a continent size garbage dumb floating in the Pacific, between Hawaii and the mainland? If all that plastic breaks up into its microscopic particles, it will kill the oceans and mankind with it. What kind of future is that?"

"We are aware of it."

"You know that global warming is caused by population growth. When you go into a public room it is designed to hold a fixed amount of people. The trains and other transportation systems can only carry certain amount of people, and I think that Earth should also have a limit. Can you scientist figure out how many people Earth can carry?"

Raymond's face light up. "It's a great ideal."

"I think the world's population is out of control, and your scientific community can have be-careful months when you try to avoid having children. It can turn into worldwide plant parenthood."

"The trouble we have is tribal needs, and the awareness just doesn't go around without enough intelligence to receive it," Raymond stated.

"Raymond I know it sounds naive but if we take care of Mother Earth, Mother Earth will take care of us."

"Yes I know," Raymond stated. "You told me that Earth is our proverbial Ark, and if we refuse to keep it in ship shape we will all go down with the wreck."

"Just figure out how many people Earth can carry," Andy said.

"I promise you as a scientist that I will figure it out."

"Your generation facing an impossible task," Andy continued. "There are people in government who don't believe in global warming."

"That's no problem, if we can't change their minds the weather will. I learned it from you, the impossible takes a little longer to do."

"I will pray for you, and I mean it."

"Thanks, we need all the help we can get," Raymond laughed.

"And I thought you were hopeless," Andy said, with a depressed smirk.

"Uncle Andy, your generation was the one who realized the problems," Raymond stated. "It takes time to switch from one energy source to another."

"But don't you think it's too late?"

"It's never too late. You told me to face my challenges not bravely but intelligently."

Suddenly everyone looked in one direction, and when Andy fallowed their gaze he saw the players were coming out of Sam's bungalow. When they came closer Andy recognized Shaquille O'Neal on front followed by Kobe Bryant, Pau Gasol, Lamar Odom, and Derek Fisher. And from another bungalow the Clippers team was streaming out with Chris Paul, Blake Griffin, DeAndre Jordan, Mat Barnes and Lamar Odom.

"My God, am I going to referee this?" Andy mumbled.

"You can handle it," Ray said, with a reassuring tap on Andy's back.

"But look at them. Just look who they are?"

"Remember what you told me."

"What the hell can I have told you that would help me now?"

"All the difficulties you go through in life will prepare you to face your final experience, with a shrug and a smile.

"How come you remember all that?"

"I wrote them down."

"You cheated."

"Uncle Andy, how many times can you referee a basketball game with real players?"

"Not many."

"It's your chance to add to your adventures."

"And make a fool of myself?"

"That's the point."

"But I never played a basketball, and I'm not sure if I know the rules. What am I going to do if something goes wrong?"

"Uncle Andy you told me many things, now let me tell you something. Our imagination dreamt up everything from gods to gasoline, figure it out."

They knuckle punched then Andy turned to gap at the players coming on to the court. The world champion Laker will play the hungry Clippers team, and Andy knew he should be a spectator and not the referee.

Andy went to meet the guys and was shaking hands when his phone rings. Andy turned away for privacy not knowing his phone was turned on speaker mode. Andy recognized Domino's minnow and he growled back. Andy had absolutely no idea that everybody was able to hear them.

"Good to hear your voice, where are you?" Andy asked.

"I'm in San Francisco," Domino said.

"What are you doing in San Francisco?"

"Talking to you and playing with my clitoris."

Andy heard the giggle and looked around to see that everyone was staring at him, and it took him a while to realize what was going on. He involuntarily dropped his jaw, jerked his hand and the phone flew from his hand, landing on the floor with the cracking sound.

"What are you going to do now, lover boy?" Sam asked, bouncing Andy a basketball. And cut the ball and watched Sam, Raymond and Melody's encouraging smiles. Standing next to them was Magic Johnson with LeBron James, and there was Steve Ballmer's beaming face.

Andy dribbled the ball a few more times because he was not sure of himself, when suddenly Cilla jumped into the screen of his mind, and hissed. Andy jumped and at the apex he lingered on long enough to flip the ball, and then he watched his twenty-five footer curved through the air and fall through the hoop, it was nothing but net. Seeing all the surprised faces Andy blew the whistle and shouted.

"LET'S PLAY BALL!"

THE END

The Obscure Concept

When I was growing up the stars in the night sky could mesmerize me and in my dreams I was among them, walking on the Milky Way.

Trudging through time we made up many theories, myths and fables about the universe and our place in it but in the absence of facts most of them are just the figments of our far-fetched imagination. There are only a few ideas worth mentioning and one of them suggests the reason for intelligent life to evolve, is to observe and verify the existence of the universe.

There are many beliefs but only one truth and in our reality where everything exists only once then it turns into something new, the possibilities are endless.

If there's an earth size planet out there with a moon to stabilize it, that planet can rotate one thousand miles an hour and the inhabitants could have a twenty four hour clock. If the planet is tilted then they have four seasons like we do, and if their planet orbits their sun at sixty-six thousand miles an hour, they might even have a 365 day calendar. When they come to realize their planet is part of a solar system within a galaxy turning more than four hundred thousand miles an hour among the billions of other galaxies then they have reached the same evolutionary stage where we are, or they have far passed us. If they are ahead of us then they have endured the struggles of our times, and learned to cure the growing pains of evolution by discarding stagnated old ideas and accepting new and exciting ones. To sharpen their adaptive skills they hold annual spring cleanings, when they would ventilate their minds from the useless old junk and leave only the antics behind.

No meter where their planet spins, it could be in our galaxy or in another one the laws of physics are the same everywhere, and as the almost evenly distributed mass of the expanding universe would indicate, it all started with a Big Burst.

According to their Big Burst Theory space-time is infinite and that space-time contains only energy, and the interaction between the two is the source of every dynamic action in the universe. As the mass of energy warps the fabric of space-time creating gravity, infinite space-time has a vacuum effect on everything made of energy, and they would call that force Dark Energy. They are also aware of the gravitational effect of Dark Matter, but they don't know if it is a substance that was the result of an interaction between space-time and energy, or it is the third substance that has always existed alongside space-time and energy and was part of the Big Burst. Of course they would know Dark Energy makes up 68.3 percent of the universe, with 26.8 percent being Dark Matter and the remaining 4.9 percent is Energy.

Their infinite space-time is like a clock that has never started and it will never stop, and this master clock has only forward motion without ever slowing down or speeding up. Everything and everyone will exist only once with a secondary clock, and when their clock stop they turn into something new. All the secondary clocks can slow down speed up or stop, but they can't go backward or go faster than the master clock.

Within infinite space-time is energy and pure energy can only form inside a singularity, where the mass of a universe is squeezed into the smallest space possible, and the pressure squashed all the fundamental particles out of existence, turning them into pure energy. The pressure inside the singularity is equal everywhere and energy in this state is massive enough to force space-time out completely, turning the singularity into a fast spinning wobbling hole, in the fabric of infinite space-time. Their Multiverse Theory claims there are as many singularities out with most of them already turned into universes, as infinite space time is. Each universe goes through their evolutionary stages and by warping the fabric of infinite space-time, they are instantaneously aware of each other.

Every rotating planet create a vortex in their surrounding fabric of space and then gravity pulls and stretches that fabric, laying it layers upon layers around the planet's surface. The accumulated layers of space-time around the planate is causing falling objects to speed up when they plunge through them, forcing them to accelerate.

A fast spinning singularity can generate a much greater vortex, and its gravity can wrap billions and billions of light years of space fabric around itself. The accumulated fabric will increase the centrifugal force and combined with all the other forces, at one point they will neutralize gravity and allow for the pressure inside the singularity to burst.

When the burst breaks up the tightly packed energy, it splits it into very fine energy strings and floods with them the billions of light years of space fabric around the singularity, accumulated there by gravity. The power of the burst blows away the forces holding it together and without gravity, the fabric of space around the singularity will bounce back into its original shape and size, carrying the attached energy strings to create a new universe. The burst of the singularity and the subsequent rebounding of space may expand into billions of light years in all directions, but it all happens within a fraction of a nanosecond.

The new universe is a rapidly expanding hot bubble and inside, the fast moving energy strings smash into each other to form photons and all the other fundamental particles, and initiating the fundamental forces to govern them. But in a dynamic cosmos nothing last forever and eventually every universe will be pulled and pushed apart by dark energy. The outspreading matter from each universe will be gathered by gravity to form six outflowing streams, and wherever the streams from six of the neighboring universes will meet, a new singularity will born. Every time the universes are dispersed and form new singularities, the Cosmos mingles and keeps infinite space-time and energy in a permanently creative state.

In this universe their concept of the cosmos is just one among the many and it doesn't matter if it's right or wrong. Without the full knowledge of the universe, most concepts are incomplete or just plain wrong. If evolution is the constant reality then eventually all reasoning life forms will learn the workings of the cosmos, not just on their own planet but everywhere where intelligent life can evolve. Every evolving individual will arrive to a level of intelligence, when they will shed their primitive survival instincts and unite under a common understanding. When everyone's intellect on a planet reaches that level their entire society can turn into an exclusive club, with everyone as an equal member.

Being the dominant species on top of the food chain, they are the guardians of their planet and would never trash their environment, or use and exploit each other like we do here on earth. They would respectfully rely on one another for the survival of all. As an integral part of this everlasting actuality they do consider reincarnation more than just a possibility and to avoid their chances to be born into the mess they have created, they all obey their prime directive for the proper care of their planet.

Without the paranoid fear of each other, their accumulated wealth can secure everyone's affluent lifestyle and keep their paradise safe from incoming meteors or comets. Their advanced technology will prepare them for the future, when their sun will turn into a red giant and their scientists have to navigate their planet to a safe distance. Guiding their planet with wisdom and adapted knowledge, they can safely sail through infinite space-time on their proverbial Ark.

The Cosmos is our awesome source of existence and it works without miracles or magic. When our spark shines in the center of infinity our outward perception defines who we are, and turns life into a spiritual experience,